SHADOWS OF CEDARVILLE

DISCLAIMER

The following work of fiction, "Shadows of Cedarville," is a product of the author's imagination. Any similarities to actual persons, places, or events are purely coincidental. The story contains elements of suspense, mystery, and the supernatural. Reader discretion is advised.

The depictions of violence, horror, and unsettling themes within this book may not be suitable for all readers. It is recommended for mature audiences who are comfortable with exploring dark and atmospheric narratives.

While the author has taken inspiration from real locations and urban legends, the portrayal of Cedarville and its inhabitants is entirely fictional. The intent is to entertain and captivate readers, rather than to accurately depict any real-world events or individuals.

Please remember that this is a work of fiction, and any beliefs or interpretations derived from the story are purely speculative. The author does not endorse or encourage any form of paranormal or supernatural activities.

Reader discretion is advised as you embark on this journey through the shadows of Cedarville.

ACKNOWLEDGMENTS

To my beloved wife Emily, and our precious children Aeva, Xander, Corissa, and Deklon, this book is dedicated to all of you, my unwavering support and the guiding light in my life. Each of you holds a piece of my heart, and it is your love and presence that inspire me to explore the depths of the unknown. Through the highs and lows, you have stood by my side, offering unwavering love, encouragement, and belief in my pursuit of truth.

Emily, your strength, compassion, and unwavering support have been the foundation on which I built my journey. Your unwavering belief in my pursuits, even in the face of the unexplainable, has given me the courage to delve deeper into the mysteries that surround us. You are my rock, and I am forever grateful for your unwavering love.

Aeva, Xander, Corissa, and Deklon, my beautiful children, you are the light that illuminates my path. Your curiosity, open minds, and unyielding spirit remind me of the importance of questioning the unknown and seeking the truth. It is with you in mind that I embark on this journey, to ensure a better future where knowledge and understanding prevail.

To everyone who has had a strange encounter and who bravely comes forward, this book is also dedicated to you. Your willingness to share your experiences, to shed light on the unexplained, is a testament to your courage and resilience. May your stories inspire others to question the mysteries that surround us and find solace in the knowledge that they are not alone.

To all those who dedicate their lives to researching and uncovering the truth, this dedication is for you. Your tireless efforts, your endless pursuit of answers, and your unwavering dedication to the realm of the unknown do not go unnoticed. You are the torchbearers, guiding us through the shadows and shedding light on the enigmas that lie before us.

May this book serve as a beacon of hope and understanding, bringing us closer to unraveling the mysteries that surround us and uniting us in our shared curiosity and quest for truth.

Remember, truth lies in the stories we share, the connections we make. Stay curious, stay open-minded. Thank you for joining us on this journey, and until next time, keep questioning, keep seeking, and keep exploring the unknown.

With deepest gratitude and love,

-Brandon

Let me in

INTRODUCTION

In the darkest corners of our world, where reality intertwines with the mysterious and the unexplained, there exist tales that defy logic and challenge our perception of what is possible. These are the stories of encounters with beings that exist beyond the realm of our understanding, leaving behind a lingering sense of fear and fascination. They are the stories that have inspired this book, serving as a haunting reminder of the unknown forces that dwell among us.

Based on real-life eyewitness accounts and the experiences of those who have dared to come forward, this book delves into the realm of the supernatural and explores the sinister nature of the encounters that have haunted individuals across the globe. While these stories are inspired by actual events, it is important to note that this book is a work of fiction, born from the twisted depths of imagination.

Within these pages, we will journey into the depths of the human psyche, where skepticism battles with curiosity, and the search for truth goes hand in hand with the fear of what lies beyond our understanding. We will encounter creatures whose existence challenges everything we thought we knew, and we will delve into the psychological and emotional impact that such encounters can have on those who experience them.

Through the eyes of our characters, we will witness the unfolding of bizarre events, the unearthing of long-buried secrets, and the relentless pursuit of answers. This book seeks to explore the true nature of these encounters, delving into the depths of the unknown and questioning the boundaries of our reality.

As we embark on this journey together, it is essential to remember that while these tales are rooted in the chilling experiences of real people, they have been molded and shaped into a work of fiction. The purpose of this book is not to claim absolute truth, but rather to provoke thought, ignite the imagination, and provide an escape into a world where the boundaries of reality are blurred.

So, dear reader, brace yourself for a descent into the shadows, where the line between fact and fiction fades, and the mysteries of the unknown beckon. Embrace the eerie tales that lie before you, and allow yourself to question the unquestionable. For within these pages, you will embark on a journey that will challenge your beliefs, stir your imagination, and leave you with a lingering sense of the enigmatic forces that surround us.

Welcome to a world where reality and fiction collide, where the truth dances with the unexplained – welcome to a realm where the bizarre encounters of the human experience unfold.

Let the journey begin.

Chapters

1   THE ENCOUNTER

Nestled on the outskirts of the sprawling Whispering Pines State Park, Cedarville, Indiana, is a place where the past wisps through the trees and the mysteries of the present are deeply rooted in the soil. Its history dates back to the early 1800s, with the land having once been an integral part of a Native American settlement. Yet, in a departure from the usual narrative, the original inhabitants left willingly, surrendering the lush, untouched landscape to the incoming settlers after several battles.

Cedarville is the epitome of a small Midwestern town, where everyone is familiar with their neighbors, and the grapevine of gossip grows as fast as the corn in July. Outsiders are rare, usually just passing through on the way to the state park, their curiosity piqued by the town's quaint charm and the subtle oddities that lurk beneath its surface.

Flanked by nature's grandeur, Cedarville has staunchly upheld its small-town ethos. The town stood resolute when big businesses attempted to make their mark, choosing to preserve their tranquility over convenience. As a result, a simple shopping trip can require a journey of over 20 miles.

With a population barely cresting 2000, Cedarville's pulse is kept alive by a collection of locally owned businesses. Among these, a paper warehouse stands solitary, just 7 miles from the town's center. This warehouse, a satellite of the lifeblood of Cedarville, the Whispering Pines Paper Company, sits in the shadows of towering trees and the secrets they keep.

The paper company, named for the state park that majestically frames the town, is the beating heart of Cedarville. It provides employment for a significant portion of the town's residents, keeping the rhythm of life steady and predictable, like the turning pages of a well-loved book. It's here where the mundane tasks of everyday life are carried out under the watchful gaze of the whispering pines. The warehouse itself, a silent sentinel, seems to hold its own mysteries, absorbed from the town and the surrounding wilderness, adding to the enigmatic charm that is Cedarville.

The paper stock warehouse was a dimly lit labyrinth of towering shelves filled with stacks of paper. The night shift crew, consisting of Bryan, Lee, Billy, Jeremiah, and Jeff, worked tirelessly amidst the hum of machinery and the aroma of freshly printed paper. They were a tight-knit group, their camaraderie forged in the crucible of long hours and shared jokes.

Their laughter echoed through the warehouse as they took a break in the small breakroom, sharing stories and ribbing each other mercilessly. Lee, a burly ex-con with a penchant for beer, teased Billy, the resident pothead jokester. Jeremiah, always the jester, had the group in fits of laughter with his endless repertoire of flatulence. Jeff, the lazy stepson of the day shift boss, James, lounged in the corner, barely contributing to the banter. And then there was Baskets, the owner's drunken, old perverted brother, who stumbled through the warehouse on occasion, his random conversations with himself adding a bizarre twist to their nights.

Their dynamic was harmonious, with one exception - Misty, the third-shift supervisor. A stern, no-nonsense woman, Misty had a reputation for being cold and demanding. Her presence was felt more in her absence, as she rarely left her office, only emerging occasionally to patrol the warehouse floor. The guys had aptly nicknamed her the "Chicken Hawk," and whenever she ventured out, they would make bird calls or noises to alert each other.

As the night wore on, the group's energy waned, exhaustion seeping into their bones. Bryan, a quiet and observant member of the crew, glanced at the clock, hoping for the end of their shift to draw near.

"Man, I can't wait to get the fuck out of here," Lee groaned, stretching his arms above his head. "I have a few cold ones waiting for me at home."

Billy chuckled, his eyes bloodshot from his earlier smoke break. "You always need a fucking cold one, Lee. I don't know how you manage to function the next day, man."

Lee shrugged, a mischievous grin on his face. "It's a talent, my friend. A talent."

Jeremiah chimed in, his voice bright with laughter. "Well, I hope you save some of that energy for the road, Lee. You never know what's lurking out there at this hour."

Bryan, ever the reserved one, nodded in agreement. "Yeah, it's always a bit creepy driving home at this hour. A lot of weird shit out there."

Jeff, who had been quiet throughout most of the conversation, finally spoke up. "I don't know what the hell you guys are talking about. I've been working here for months and I've never seen anything strange on my way home."

Billy chuckled and nudged Jeff playfully. "That's because you're too busy sleeping in the breakroom, Jeffrey. You wouldn't notice if a fucking UFO landed right in front of you."

The group erupted in laughter, the tension of the night momentarily forgotten. Even Bryan cracked a smile, appreciating the light-hearted banter that helped ease the monotony of their long shifts.

As the clock struck 4:45 AM, Misty emerged from her office, surprising everyone with a rare act of leniency. "Alright, guys, James is on vacation this week, so I guess I can let you all go home a little early. Don't make a habit of it though."

The crew cheered, their energy renewed at the prospect of leaving the warehouse sooner than usual. They gathered their belongings and bid farewell to Baskets, who was already dozing off in a corner.

Outside, the air felt crisp and still. The parking lot, usually bustling with the cars of their coworkers, was empty and eerily quiet. The absence of their usual companions added an extra layer of unease to the night.

Bryan, unlocking his 1998 Ford Explorer, looked over at Billy, who was climbing into his old 1990's Chevy Silverado. "Hey man, are you good? Do you want to follow me? It's always better to stick together, especially at this hour, and with you being fucked up."

Billy chuckled, patting the worn-out roof of his truck. "Nah man, I've got my trusty steed here. Don't worry about me, I'll be fine."

Bryan shrugged, understanding Billy's stubbornness. "Alright, dude. Just be careful out there. You know how weird things can get on these late-night drives. Lots of deer and shit out and about."

With a wave and a playful beep of the horn, Bryan started his engine and pulled out of the parking lot, leaving Billy behind. The road stretched out before him, the only source of light being the dim glow of his headlights.

As he drove, Bryan couldn't shake off the feeling of being watched. His eyes constantly darted to the rearview mirror, searching for any sign of movement. The shadows seemed to dance at the periphery of Bryan's vision, taunting him with their mysterious movements. His grip on the steering wheel tightened, his knuckles turning white. The road ahead seemed to stretch on forever, even if it was only a few miles, the isolation amplifying his unease.

Bryan turned down a county road and noticed a car was a little ways in front of him. The red taillights, his only sign to alert him of its presence, illuminated on the roadway. As Bryan inched closer to the vehicle, he realized it was Lee, as he drove his 1980's Chevy Chevette. Bryan followed closely behind Lee's car, their headlights cutting through the darkness like twin beacons. The weariness from the long day settled over him, and he wondered why Lee had suddenly swerved off the road. Concern flickered in his mind as he watched his friend's taillights disappear into the distance.

As Bryan approached the spot where Lee had veered off, his eyes widened in horror. There, in the glow of his headlights, stood a tall, black figure. The headless and armless torso swayed unnaturally, defying the laws of human movement. Fear tightened its grip around Bryan's heart, urging him to drive away, to escape the unimaginable horror before him. But as he hit the brakes, his car screeching to a halt, the creature passed by his driver's window, its towering presence sending a wave of terror crashing over him.

It stood over seven feet tall, its hunched form leaning forward as if burdened by some unseen weight. The absence of a head or arms sent a chill down Bryan's spine, and he couldn't tear his eyes away from the grotesque sight.

With a surge of adrenaline, Bryan slammed his foot on the accelerator, his tires spinning against the pavement as he raced away from the nightmarish encounter. The image of the headless figure haunted his mind as he desperately searched for Lee's car. Finally spotting Lee's vehicle pulled into an abandoned gravel driveway, Bryan's heart pounded with a mix of relief and trepidation. He parked his Explorer next to Lee's car and rushed out, his limbs trembling with fear and anticipation.

Lee, his face pale and eyes wide with terror, stumbled out of his car, his words tumbling out in a panicked rush. "Crazy! Did you see it? It didn't have a fucking head! It was just... walking... Oh God, what the hell was that?"

Taking a deep breath to steady himself, Bryan made a decision that defied logic. "We have to go back, man. We have to find out what that thing was."

Lee's eyes widened in disbelief. "Are you fucking stupid? We need to get the fuck out of here!"

But Bryan's curiosity outweighed his fear. He felt an inexplicable need to confront the unknown, to understand the nature of the horrifying creature they had encountered. Ignoring Lee's protests, he turned back towards the road, his resolve firm.

As they retraced their path, his headlights casting long, eerie shadows along the road, a heavy silence settled over him. The air felt charged with an unsettling energy, as if the very essence of the night had shifted. Bryan's heart pounded in his chest, his senses on high alert, as he ventured deeper into the unknown.

Suddenly, the Explorer's headlights illuminated a massive shape sprawled across the road. Bryan's breath caught in his throat as he caught sight of the creature. It was like something out of a nightmare, a twisted fusion of man and beast. The creature lay there, its matted fur blending seamlessly with the darkness. Its powerful frame was hunched, its muscles coiled with an otherworldly strength. The yellow glow of its eyes pierced through the night, reflecting an intelligence that sent a shiver down Bryan's spine.

As Bryan cautiously stepped out of the Explorer, his eyes locked with those piercing, glowing orbs. The creature's head lifted, revealing a mouth filled with razor-sharp teeth, glistening menacingly in the faint moonlight. In that moment, time seemed to stand still as the growl that emanated from deep within its throat reverberated through the stillness of the night.

Fear gripped Bryan, freezing him in place. Every instinct screamed at him to run, to flee from the monstrous creature before him. But a morbid fascination held him captive, his eyes locked with the creature's intense gaze.

With a slow, deliberate movement, the creature rose to its full height, towering over Bryan. Its body rippled with unnatural strength, muscles bulging beneath its coarse fur. A chilling smile curled across its lupine face, revealing rows of gleaming fangs.

A primal terror washed over Bryan as the creature's gaze locked onto him with an unsettling intensity. It seemed to see into his very soul, as if it knew his deepest fears and darkest secrets. The realization that he was in the presence of something beyond comprehension gripped him, threatening to consume his sanity.

Just as Bryan thought he couldn't bear the tension any longer, the creature lowered itself back down with an eerie grace. In a flash, it turned and darted off into the surrounding woods, disappearing into the shadows as quickly as it had arrived.

As Bryan stood there, his body still trembling from the encounter with the Dogman creature, he heard the sound of Lee's car door slam shut. Lee stumbled out of his vehicle, his face contorted with a mix of disbelief and terror. He let out a string of expletives, his voice filled with raw panic.

"What the fuck was that, Crazy? How is any of this even possible?" Lee's voice wavered as he struggled to make sense of the nightmarish events they had just witnessed.

Bryan turned to face Lee, his own mind reeling with the same questions. "I have no fucking idea, man. But we can't stay here. There's something deeply wrong about this place."

As they huddled together, their voices hushed and filled with a mixture of fear and confusion, Bryan's gaze shifted to the ground between them. There, standing on its hind legs, was a small mouse. It cleaned itself with meticulous precision, seemingly unaffected by the chaos surrounding them.

With a mixture of curiosity and terror, Bryan nudged the mouse with his foot. It didn't scurry away like a typical rodent would; instead, it continued its grooming ritual, undeterred by his presence. The sight sent a chill down his spine, adding to the growing sense of unease that hung in the air.

Lee and Bryan exchanged a glance, their wide eyes mirroring each other's disbelief. The night air felt crisp and unsettling, the silence of the surrounding area amplifying their fears. They knew they couldn't stay any longer in this nightmarish realm. In silent agreement, they made their way back to their respective vehicles. The engines roared to life, breaking the eerie stillness that had engulfed the area. Lee and Bryan drove down the road together, their minds racing with the inexplicable horrors they had encountered.

At the point where the road split, Lee veered off in one direction, his taillights fading into the distance. Bryan took a deep breath, his grip on the steering wheel tightening. He turned his car in the opposite direction, determined to put as much distance as possible between himself and the nightmarish realm they had just left behind.

As he drove, the events of the night replayed in his mind, each scene etching itself into his memory. The road stretched out before him, illuminated by the faint glow of his headlights. The night was far from over, and Bryan knew that the terrors they had witnessed were just the beginning.

As Bryan pulled into his driveway, his mind buzzing with unanswered questions, he knew he had to find some semblance of understanding. Determined, he hurried inside his house and turned on his computer, the screen casting an eerie glow across his face.

He delved into the depths of the internet, desperately searching for any information that could shed light on the creature they had encountered. Page after page, he scoured through werewolf lore and cryptid sightings, until he stumbled upon a forum dedicated to Dogman encounters. The stories he found sent a chill down his spine, resonating eerily with his own experience.

Eager to document his encounter, Bryan grabbed a sketchbook and a pencil. His hands trembled as he painstakingly recreated the monstrous visage of the Dogman, capturing every haunting detail. The more he sketched, the more he felt a connection with the countless others who claimed to have seen the same creature.

Driven by an insatiable need for answers, Bryan couldn't contain his excitement. Only two days later, he returned to work, determined to share his discoveries with his colleagues. As he approached his coworkers, excitement dancing in his eyes, their laughter erupted through the office.

"What's up, Bryan? Still obsessing over that werewolf bullshit?" one of his coworkers sneered, his laughter echoing through the break room.

Lee's face contorted with frustration and embarrassment. He sidled up to Bryan, his voice a harsh whisper. "Damn it, Crazy! I told you to drop it! We can't afford to have people thinking we're fucking lunatics."

Bryan's heart sank, his excitement replaced with disappointment. "But dude, we saw it! We experienced it together!"

Lee's eyes narrowed, his voice laced with anger. "I don't care! I don't want people making fun of us or thinking we're insane. If you keep talking about this shit, I'll deny it ever fucking happened. They'll believe me over you. Everyone already calls you 'Crazy' for a reason."

Bryan's shoulders slumped, the weight of his friend's words settling upon him. It was clear that Lee wanted nothing to do with the terrifying encounter they had shared. Reluctantly, Bryan made the decision to keep his experience to himself, burying it deep within, until around 15 years later when the haunting memories would resurface.

2   SHADOWS OF THE PAST

It was another exhausting day on the construction site for Bryan Roberts. As the sun began to set and the sounds of hammers and machinery faded into the background, he couldn't wait to return home to the comfort of his family.

Bryan's tires crunched against the gravel as he pulled into the driveway of his modest home in Cedarville. The day had been long, filled with the usual demands of his job as a construction project supervisor. But today, as he stepped out of his car and glanced up at the darkening sky, the weight of the years pressed heavily upon him. Fifteen years had passed since that first encounter, since the strange creature walking had shattered his perception of the world.

In the wake of that chilling experience, Bryan had made a choice, a choice to keep the truth hidden deep within him. It was a secret burden he had carried alone, far from the prying eyes of his family and friends.

Laney, his loving wife, had sensed the change in him over the years. She had witnessed the moments when he withdrew into himself, his eyes clouded with a haunted look. But she knew better than to pry, to question the depths of his silence. And so, the secret remained locked away, festering in the shadows of their shared existence.

As he walked through the front door, the familiar sounds of laughter and chaos greeted his ears. His wife, Laney, was in the living room, her face lighting up as their four children - Eva, Alek, Clarissa, and Declan - ran around, their energy seemingly boundless.

Bryan leaned against the hallway wall, watching the scene with a mixture of exhaustion and love. He couldn't help but smile as he caught Laney's eye, silently acknowledging the beautiful chaos that was their life.

Laney, a strong and compassionate woman, approached him with a knowing look. "Long day, huh?"

Bryan nodded, rubbing the back of his neck. "You have no idea. But hey, it's worth it. All of this," he gestured to the bustling living room, "is what keeps me going."

Laney wrapped her arms around him, her warmth and support grounding him. "I'm proud of you, you know? For following your passion with the podcast, even if it means late nights in the basement."

Bryan chuckled, thinking about the hours he spent researching and recording his episodes after the kids were sound asleep. "Yeah, I never saw myself as a believer in all this supernatural stuff. But that first encounter... it changed everything."

Laney's eyes softened, her voice filled with understanding. "I know. And you're doing important work, Bryan. Shedding light on things that most people ignore or dismiss. Just be careful, okay? I worry about you out there."

Bryan nodded, his gaze drifting to the family photos on the wall. "I promise, I'll be careful. For you and the kids."

As they stood there, finding solace in each other's embrace, Bryan knew that the journey ahead would be treacherous. But with his family by his side, he felt a renewed sense of purpose.

As the evening settled in, Bryan found himself lost in his thoughts, the events of that fateful day replaying in his mind with vivid clarity. The strange creature walking, the Dogman lurking in the shadows, it all seemed so surreal, as if ripped from the pages of a horror novel. But he knew, deep down, that it was all too real.

In the depths of the night, as sleep eluded him once more, Bryan gazed out of the bedroom window. The moonlight cast an ethereal glow upon the landscape, its silver beams revealing a landscape on the outskirts of Whispering Pines State Park. An eerie calmness surrounded the woods.

It was a lazy Sunday morning, the sun streaming through the windows as the Roberts family gathered around the breakfast table. The aroma of freshly brewed coffee filled the air, mingling with the sound of laughter and clinking cutlery. Bryan sat at the head of the table, a content smile on his face as he watched his children devour pancakes and share stories from their week. Laney sat beside him, her hand resting gently on his knee, a silent support in a chaotic world.

"So, Daddy," Clarissa, their youngest daughter, piped up, her eyes sparkling with curiosity. "Are there any new Dogman stories for your podcast?"

Bryan chuckled, taking a sip of his coffee. "Oh, you bet, Sweet pea. I've got some chilling ones lined up for the next episode. You won't believe the encounters people have had."

Alek, their oldest son, leaned forward, his interest piqued. "Do you think they're real, Dad? These Dogman things?"

Bryan paused for a moment, his gaze shifting to Laney before he answered. "Well, son, I used to be a skeptic just like you. But after that first encounter, I can't deny that there's something out there. Something dangerous. And it's my job to uncover the truth."

Eva, their oldest, chimed in. "But Dad, isn't it scary? I mean, what if you come face-to-face with one of those creatures?"

Bryan's expression softened as he reached across the table, taking Eva's hand in his. "I won't lie, Eva. It's terrifying. But I do this because I want to protect people. I want to make sure no one else has to go through what we went through."

Laney nodded, her voice filled with pride. "Your father is brave, kids. He's willing to face the unknown to keep others safe. We're lucky to have him."

The room fell into a comfortable silence as the family savored their breakfast, each lost in their own thoughts. In that moment, Bryan felt a surge of gratitude for the love and support that surrounded him, giving him the strength to face the horrors that awaited him in his investigations. Fifteen years had come and gone, but the memory of that fateful night still haunted Bryan's every waking moment. The encounter with the Dogman creature had left an indelible mark on his soul, igniting a relentless curiosity that refused to be extinguished.

Driven by an insatiable need for answers, Bryan had spent years delving into the world of the supernatural and unexplained. His nighttime hobby as a podcaster provided him with the perfect platform to explore the realm of the unknown. Armed with a microphone and a burning determination, Bryan created *Beastly Encounters* as he set out to uncover the truth behind the strange events that had unfolded that eerie night.

His podcast gained traction, attracting a growing audience of believers and skeptics alike. Bryan's reputation as an astute investigator of the paranormal grew, and his interviews with eyewitnesses of cryptid encounters became a cornerstone of his show. With each conversation, Bryan sought to piece together the fragmented puzzle of that unforgettable night. He delved into the stories of those who had come face to face with creatures like the Dogman, drawing parallels and connecting the dots between their experiences and his own.

Bryan sat in his dimly lit basement studio, surrounded by files and notes on the Dogman phenomenon. The microphone in front of him hummed with anticipation as he prepared for his next episode of *Beastly Encounters*.

Laney descended the basement stairs, a concerned look on her face. "Bryan, I can't shake this feeling of dread. Are you sure you want to keep going with this? It's getting scarier every day."

Bryan's eyes flickered with a mix of determination and fear. "Laney, I understand your concerns, but we can't let fear hold us back. The truth needs to be told. People have a right to know what's out there."

She sighed, her voice filled with worry. "But what if these people are crazy? What happens if they come after us? What if everyone thinks you're crazy too? There's just so many questions, and I just worry about you."

Bryan's voice dropped to a low whisper. "That's a risk we have to take. If we stop now, we'll be letting fear win. We have to keep going, for the sake of all those who have encountered these horrors. I've been careful about who I allow to our house, and these people check out."

Laney's eyes glistened with tears. "I just don't want to lose you, Bryan. I can't bear the thought of something happening to you, or what this may do to the children. People can't always be trusted."

Bryan reached out, gripping her trembling hands. "I understand your fear, Laney. But I promise you, I won't let anything happen to us. I'll be cautious, I'll be smart. We'll face this together. If anyone were to try something, then they clearly don't know who they're fucking with."

Bryan sat across from Dr. Samantha Collins in his makeshift recording studio. The room was bathed in warm, golden light, casting gentle shadows on the walls. The anticipation crackled in the air as they prepared to embark on a profound conversation about the trauma experienced by those who had encountered strange creatures. Adjusting his microphone, Bryan leaned forward, his eyes filled with both curiosity and empathy.

"Welcome to the show, Dr. Collins," he said, his voice laced with genuine warmth. "I am truly grateful to have you here today. Your expertise in this field is invaluable. Could you please share a bit about your background and your personal experience with these creatures?"

Dr. Collins settled into her chair, her posture erect and her eyes focused. There was a quietness in her voice as she began to speak. "Thank you, Bryan. My journey in this field began with a haunting encounter during my childhood. I was a teenager and it was just another tranquil camping trip with my family, surrounded by the beauty of nature. But one night, as darkness descended upon our campsite, our entire world was shattered."

Her hands trembled slightly as she continued, her gaze fixed on a distant memory. "Tall, canine-like creatures emerged from the shadows, their eyes glowing with an otherworldly ferocity. Chaos erupted as fear gripped us. We fought tooth and nail to escape their clutches, and by some miraculous stroke of luck, we managed to flee unharmed. The campsite, however, was torn to shreds."

Bryan leaned forward, captivated by her story. His eyes widened, reflecting a mix of curiosity and compassion. "That must have been an unimaginable ordeal for you and your family. How did that experience shape your decision to work with trauma victims who have encountered similar phenomena?"

Dr. Collins nodded, her expression grave yet resolute. "It was a defining moment, Bryan. Witnessing those creatures firsthand made me acutely aware of the profound psychological impact such encounters can have. In the aftermath, I felt a calling to dedicate my life to understanding and helping others who had faced similar terrors. I wanted to create a safe haven for them, a place where they could find solace and healing."

Bryan's eyes flickered with admiration as he absorbed her words. "It's disheartening to hear that there is often skepticism surrounding these accounts. Why do you think people are hesitant to come forward with their experiences?"

Dr. Collins sighed, her voice tinged with a hint of sadness. "Society has a tendency to dismiss the unexplained, Bryan. Those who come forward with stories of encountering these creatures are met with raised eyebrows and skepticism. The fear of being labeled as delusional or attention-seeking often silences their voices, leaving them to suffer in isolation."

Bryan furrowed his brow, a mixture of concern and frustration evident on his face. "That's truly unfortunate. How can we, as a society, create a more supportive environment for these individuals to share their stories?"

Dr. Collins leaned forward, her eyes filled with determination. "It starts with empathy, Bryan. We need to actively listen to their experiences without judgment or preconceived notions. By validating their emotions and acknowledging the courage it takes to share such deeply personal and often traumatic encounters, we can create a safe space for them to express themselves."

Bryan's eyes sparkled with understanding as he absorbed her words. "Absolutely. So, what steps can we take to break down the stigma surrounding these encounters and provide validation for those who have experienced them?"

Dr. Collins took a deep breath, her voice steady and resolute. "Education is key, Bryan. We must raise awareness about the psychological impact of these encounters and challenge the prevailing skepticism. By sharing the stories of survivors, we can humanize their experiences and foster a sense of understanding. It is crucial to create an environment where individuals feel empowered to come forward without fear of ridicule or disbelief."

Bryan nodded, a sense of purpose emanating from him. "I couldn't agree more, Dr. Collins. It is essential that we strive for empathy, understanding, and education to support those who have encountered these creatures and ensure their voices are heard."

Dr. Collins smiled, a glimmer of hope in her eyes. "Indeed, Bryan. Together, we can all make a difference and provide solace to those who have faced these unimaginable encounters. It begins with the power of dialogue and the willingness to listen. As a society, we are too quick to judge. Maybe not everyone is being completely honest, but I don't believe everyone is lying either."

Bryan leaned back in his chair, a sense of awe and inspiration washing over him. He couldn't help but be moved by Dr. Collins' unwavering dedication and the profound impact she was making in the lives of trauma victims. It was clear that her passion ran deep, and her words had struck a chord within him.

"I am truly grateful for the work you are doing, Dr. Collins," Bryan said, his voice filled with admiration. "Your commitment to helping those who have encountered these creatures is truly remarkable. What do you hope to achieve through your research and support?"

Dr. Collins took a moment to collect her thoughts, her gaze focused and resolute. "My ultimate goal, Bryan, is to provide a sense of healing and closure to trauma victims. By delving into their experiences, understanding the psychological impact, and offering tailored support, I aim to guide them towards a path of recovery. I want them to know that they are not alone, that their encounters are valid, and that there is hope for healing and regaining control over their lives."

Bryan nodded, his eyes shining with a newfound sense of purpose. "That's incredibly inspiring, Dr. Collins. How can individuals who have encountered these creatures, or those who know someone who has, seek the support and resources you provide?"

Dr. Collins leaned forward, a compassionate smile gracing her lips. "There are various avenues for support, Bryan. I have established a network of professionals, including therapists and support groups, who specialize in trauma related to these encounters. Additionally, my research has led to the development of resources and online communities where individuals can connect and share their experiences in a safe and understanding environment. It's essential to reach out, to seek support, and to know that help is available."

Bryan felt a surge of gratitude for Dr. Collins' tireless efforts. Her words resonated deeply within him, and he knew that he had a role to play in amplifying the message of hope and understanding.

"Thank you, Dr. Collins," he said earnestly. "Your work is not only changing lives but also challenging societal norms. Through this conversation, I hope to shed light on the importance of empathy, validation, and support for those who have encountered these creatures. To my listeners out there, together, we can make a difference."

Dr. Collins nodded, her eyes shining with gratitude. "Indeed, Bryan. Together, we can create a world where the experiences of trauma victims are acknowledged and embraced with compassion. I am grateful for this opportunity to share my journey and spread awareness about the psychological impact of these encounters. It is my hope that by shining a light on these stories, we can foster a greater sense of understanding and empathy within society."

As their conversation drew to a close, Bryan couldn't help but feel a renewed sense of purpose. He knew that this conversation would serve as a catalyst for change, igniting a spark within listeners to challenge their preconceptions and support those who have faced these extraordinary encounters.

Brandon Wright © 2023

In the days that followed, Bryan meticulously edited the recording of their conversation. His words flowed with a sense of reverence, capturing the essence of the profound conversation that had taken place.

Finally, the episode was ready for release. Bryan took a moment to reflect on the power of storytelling, knowing that through his podcast, he had the ability to touch the hearts and minds of countless individuals. He pressed the "publish" button, sending their conversation out into the world.

And as listeners tuned in, they were transported into the intimate space of that recording studio, feeling the weight of the words and the depth of the emotions conveyed. They were captivated by the descriptive body language, the detailed accounts, and the unwavering determination of Dr. Collins.

In the days that followed, Bryan received an outpouring of messages from listeners who had been deeply moved by the conversation. Some shared their own encounters, finding comfort in knowing they were not alone. Others expressed their understanding and pledged to be more supportive of those who had faced similar traumas.

On the next episode of *Beastly Encounters*, Bryan introduces his guest, Dr. Abby Turner, a renowned cryptozoologist who has extensively researched the Dogman phenomenon. As they delve into the topic, Dr. Turner shares bone-chilling stories of encounters with these creatures in state parks and nature preserves.

Dr. Turner's voice quivers with trepidation as she recounts a particularly terrifying encounter. "I was deep in the forest, studying wildlife, when I saw it. A dark, hulking figure lurking in the shadows. Its eyes glowed with an otherworldly intensity, and a primal fear gripped me."

Bryan's voice trembles as he asks, "And what did it do?"

Dr. Turner's voice drops to a hushed whisper. "It stared at me, as if it could see right through me. Then, it let out a bloodcurdling howl that seemed to pierce my very soul. I knew I had stumbled upon a sacred territory, a place where humans were not meant to tread. Its growls reverberated through the trees, sending a shiver down my spine. I had to escape, to get as far away as possible."

Bryan's voice quivered as he pressed further. "Did it chase after you?"

Dr. Turner's breath hitched as she replied, her voice filled with dread. "Oh, it did. Its heavy footsteps echoed behind me, gaining speed with each passing moment. I could feel its hot breath on the back of my neck, its presence closing in. It was like a predator hunting its prey."

The episode ended abruptly, leaving the listeners in a state of heightened fear and anticipation. Bryan explained that occasionally there were issues with internet connections when you discuss Dogman encounters. Other podcasters have had similar instances he explained. This continued to add mystique to the ever-growing mysteries of these strange creatures. The realization of the true horrors lurking within the Dogman phenomenon weighed heavily on the listeners minds. The suspense was palpable, as each listener wondered if they, too, would encounter these terrifying creatures one day.

As *Beastly Encounters* gained popularity, an atmosphere of unease settled over the listeners. The stories grew darker, the encounters more menacing. Bryan's commitment to exposing the truth pushed him deeper into the unknown, while Laney's worry for his safety intensified. The lines between reality and the supernatural blurred, leaving everyone wondering if they were truly safe from the clutches of the evil that resides around them.

As Bryan sat in his basement studio, his heart pounding with anticipation. Today's episode of *Beastly Encounters* would be the most chilling yet. He took a deep breath and adjusted his headphones, preparing to introduce his next guest.

The room was filled with an eerie silence as Bryan spoke into the microphone. "Welcome back, listeners, to another new episode of *Beastly Encounters*. Today, we have a special guest on call with us who survived a terrifying encounter with what he believes to be Dogmen in the remote woods in the state of Washington. Please join me in welcoming Eric Thompson to the show."

The air crackled with anticipation as Eric's voice filled through Bryan's headphones. "Thank you for having me on, Bryan. It's not easy to talk about what happened, but I believe people need to know the truth."

Bryan's voice was filled with curiosity and empathy as he asked, "It's my pleasure, man. Now Eric, can you take us back to that fateful night in the woods? What exactly did you witness?"

Eric's voice quivered as he relived the horrifying memories. "I was camping with my buddies in a state park in Washington. Late into the night, we heard screams coming from the neighboring campsite. At first, we thought it was just a large bear, but when I saw the creatures illuminated by the campfire, I knew it was something else entirely."

Bryan leaned forward, his voice filled with both fascination and concern. "What did you see, Eric? Can you describe these creatures for the audience?"

Eric took a deep breath, his voice filled with a mixture of fear and conviction. "Bryan, I saw a pack of upright walking creatures that resembled werewolves. They looked like what you see in these scary movies. They were tall, with sharp teeth and glowing yellowish eyes. It was like something straight out of a nightmare."

The gravity of Eric's words hung in the air as Bryan pressed further. "And what happened after you saw these creatures? How did you manage to escape?"

Eric's voice wavered as he recounted the harrowing escape. "When we heard the screams, man, we knew we had to get the fuck out of there. We quickly got into the truck and drove away, leaving the whole terrifying scene behind us. I still have nightmares about it to this day."

Bryan nodded, his voice filled with empathy. "Thank you, Eric, for sharing your story. I know the toll it takes, and that it takes immense courage to speak about such traumatic experiences. I truly appreciate you sharing that with us."

Bryan concluded Eric's episode, leaving listeners on the edge of their seats.

As the next installment of *Beastly Encounters* began, he introduced his new guest, Kyle Mason, an expert in the phenomenon of missing people in national parks.

"Tonight I would like to welcome my next guest, Kyle," Bryan greeted, his voice filled with anticipation. " Kyle, I'm thrilled to have you on the show today. Your research on the disappearances in national parks is truly fascinating, and you also believe it ties into the Dogman mystery we've been exploring."

Kyle's voice resonated through the speakers, filled with a mix of concern and intrigue. "Thank you, Bryan. It's an honor to be here. For years now, I've been investigating the strange cases of missing people in national parks, and what I've discovered is both chilling and perplexing."

Bryan leaned forward, eager to hear more. "Please, Kyle, share your findings with us."

Kyle took a deep breath, his words measured and thoughtful. "There's a pattern in these disappearances. People go missing without a trace, no signs of struggle or any indication of what happened to them. It's as if they vanish into thin air. And when we examine the locations where these disappearances occur, they often coincide with areas where Dogman sightings have been reported."

A shiver ran down Bryan's spine as he processed the implications of Kyle's words. "Are you suggesting that these Dogmen creatures have the ability to appear and disappear into our reality? Like they are somehow linked to these mysterious disappearances?"

Kyle's voice grew more urgent. "Yes, that's what I believe. There have been numerous accounts of witnesses seeing these bizarre creatures seemingly materialize out of nowhere or simply vanish without explanation. It's as if they possess the ability to move between dimensions or blur the boundaries of our reality."

The implications of what Kyle was suggesting were mind-boggling. It opened up a realm of possibilities that Bryan had only scratched the surface of in his research. The Dogman phenomenon was no longer just about cryptids or legends. It was entangled in a web of disappearances, unexplained phenomena, and a reality that was far stranger than anyone could have imagined.

"Bryan, it's truly baffling," Kyle began. "In my investigations, I've analyzed countless reports of missing individuals, and the patterns are undeniable. These disappearances occur in remote areas, often without any witnesses or evidence left behind. There are no signs of struggle, no footprints, and no trace of the missing person. It's as if they've vanished into thin air."

Bryan's curiosity grew with each word, his mind racing to comprehend the implications. "And how does this tie into the Dogman phenomenon?" he asked, eager to connect the dots.

Kyle took a deep breath, his voice tinged with conviction. "Based on my research and the accounts I've collected, I believe these Dogman creatures possess the ability to exist in multiple dimensions. They can seamlessly move between our reality and another, allowing them to appear and disappear at will."

He continued, painting a vivid picture of interdimensional beings with a profound impact on the world around them. "Imagine a scenario where a person unknowingly stumbles upon a portal or a gateway between dimensions. If a Dogman happens to be nearby, it could seize the opportunity to cross over, snatching the individual and whisking them away into another realm, leaving no trace behind."

Bryan's mind raced with the implications of this theory. It explained the lack of evidence, the absence of any logical explanation for the disappearances. The missing people had unwittingly become intertwined in a realm beyond their understanding, caught in the crosshairs of interdimensional creatures.

As the episode neared its end, Bryan couldn't contain his gratitude for Kyle's insightful contributions. He thanked him for joining the show and sharing his extensive research and beliefs.

"Kyle, I can't thank you enough for being here today and shedding light on these fascinating theories," Bryan expressed sincerely. "Your dedication and passion for uncovering the truth are truly inspiring. I'm honored to have had you as a guest on *Beastly Encounters*."

Kyle humbly acknowledged the appreciation. "Thank you, Bryan. It's been a pleasure to be a part of this conversation and share my findings. Together, we're making progress in unraveling the mysteries that surround us."

Bryan shifted his focus to the audience, "To all our listeners, I want to assure you that our quest for truth will continue. We won't stop until we've explored every avenue, uncovered every hidden detail. The missing people and the Dogman phenomenon deserve our unwavering dedication."

He continued, his excitement palpable. "Now, I'm thrilled to announce that our next guest on *Beastly Encounters* is a man named John. He has a unique perspective and his own experiences to share. I can't wait for you all to join us for the upcoming episode."

As the episode drew to a close, Bryan signed off with his usual saying to his audience. "Remember, truth lies in the stories we share, the connections we make. Stay curious, stay open-minded. Thank you for joining us on this journey, and until next time, keep questioning, keep seeking, and keep exploring the unknown."

With those final words, the episode concluded, leaving the audience eagerly anticipating the next installment of *Beastly Encounters* and the insights that John would bring to the table.

In the highly anticipated interview with John, *Beastly Encounters* delved into the chilling encounter that had haunted him for years. As Bryan sat at his desk waiting for the call from John, the atmosphere was thick with anticipation, the room seemingly holding its breath, ready to hear the unsettling details.

With a deep breath, John began to recount the night that had forever changed his life. His voice was filled with a mix of fear and nervousness to share his truth.

"It was a cold, moonless night, about eight years ago," John began, his eyes seemingly lost in the memory. "I was alone in my house, it was pretty quiet outside, the silence broken only by the distant sound of wind rustling through the trees. I heard what sounded like a tapping on glass, and that's when I saw it. This creature, this hellish abomination, wash standing outside my front window, its eyes gleaming with a yellow whitish glow."

Bryan leaned in, captivated by John's words, his eyes reflecting a mix of concern and intrigue. "What did it look like, John? What sort of details can you remember?" he asked, his voice steady yet laced with a hint of unease.

John's voice quivered as he continued, "It had the body of a massive wolf, standing upright on two legs, but its features were twisted and grotesque. Its fur was matted, as if it hadn't seen a moment of care, and its teeth, oh Jesus, its teeth were sharp and stained with blood. It was like it had just eaten something. But it was its eyes, Bryan, its eyes that scared the shit out of me. They pierced through my soul, as if it could see every dark secret, every hidden fear within me. I know that doesn't make any sense, but that's how it felt, Bryan. This thing just felt... I don't know how else to describe it."

As John spoke, the room seemed to grow colder, the air thick with an unspoken terror. Bryan, his heart pounding, pressed on, determined to understand the full extent of John's harrowing experience.

"That's okay, John. Please, what happened next?" Bryan asked, his voice barely above a whisper.

John's voice trembled as he continued, his eyes filled with a mixture of fear and defiance. "This next part is going to sound fucking ridiculous, but it spoke to me, Bryan. Not with its mouth, but directly into my fucking mind. The voice, it echoed through my thoughts, demanding that I 'let it in.' Its words were laced with a malevolence that sent shivers down my spine."

Bryan leaned forward, "And what did you do, John?"

Fear etched in every line of his face, John replied "Bryan, I was paralyzed with fear," John confessed, his voice quivering. "I couldn't bring myself to move, I was just frozen, staring at that abomination outside my home. I was finally able to move, so I ran to another room, hoping to escape its grasp on my mind."

Bryan nodded, his eyes filled with empathy. "I can't even imagine the terror you must have felt, John. To have something so menacing, so otherworldly, invade your sanctuary."

John's voice strained with the weight of his memories. "But even as I hid, the creature's presence lingered, tormenting me. Its voice, like a sinister echo, continued to resound in my mind, mocking my fear, my prayers, my faith. It knew my weakness, Bryan, and it reveled in it. I just hid in my room, hearing scratches along the walls."

Bryan's brow furrowed in deep contemplation. "John, what you experienced, the way it taunted you when you prayed, it's unsettling. It almost suggests a darker, more malevolent nature to these creatures. A connection to the demonic, perhaps."

A shiver ran down John's spine, his eyes widening with realization. "You might be onto something, Bryan. I've often thought about the way it mocked my prayers, the way it seemed to revel in my fear. It felt...evil. Like it was playing with me, toying with my soul. It wanted me to be afraid. It wanted me to know I was weak."

As the weight of their conversation settled around them, a shared understanding filled the room. The encounter John had with the Dogman-like creature, and the sinister nature of its telepathic communication, seemed to align with a deeper, more malevolent force at play.

Bryan's voice broke the heavy silence, his words carrying a mixture of caution and resolve. "John, your experience, the way it unfolded, it's a chilling reminder that these creatures, whatever they may be, are not to be taken lightly. They pose a threat, not just physically, but on a spiritual level as well. I personally recommend anyone listening to proceed with caution if you try to investigate these sorts of things."

John nodded, a determined glint in his eyes. "You're right, Bryan. We can't dismiss this as mere folklore or imagination. There's something truly sinister about these encounters, something that goes beyond the realm of the natural. I believe they are pure evil, and no one should be stupid enough to try and find these things. Trust me, you don't want to find these things."

As the interview concluded, a sense of unease lingered in the air. The realization that these creatures may indeed possess a malevolent nature cast a dark shadow over the mind of Bryan. The path he had embarked upon was a treacherous one, but one that he was still determined to tread.

3   SURVIVORS GUILT

As the podcast continued to grow, one interview led to another, each conversation unveiling new pieces of the supernatural tapestry. The tales of horror and inexplicable phenomena became the fabric of Bryan's existence, weaving a web of intrigue that both terrified and exhilarated him.

One night, as he sat in his makeshift podcast studio, Bryan couldn't ignore the nagging voice in his head any longer. It was time to reveal his own story, to lay bare the events that had forever changed his life.

With a deep breath, he began recording, recounting the harrowing encounter with the Dogman creature, sparing no detail. The words flowed from his lips, a mixture of fear, fascination, and longing for understanding. Through the microphone, he poured out his heart, sharing the depths of his emotions with his listeners.

As the episode aired, the response was overwhelming. Messages flooded in from those who resonated with Bryan's story, who had experienced similar encounters or shared his insatiable curiosity. They offered support, validation, and their own tales of the unexplained.

But amidst the flood of acceptance, there were pockets of skepticism, voices dismissing Bryan's account as lies, or misidentification.

His story gained attention locally, which attracted a man named Tony Baker, who reached out to Bryan to be a guest on the podcast. Tony had an encounter back in 1990, and he's withheld it for over 30 years, but now is willing to come forward.

Born in the early 1970s, Tony has become an emblem of time's relentless march and the trials it leaves in its wake. Now in his 50s, he is a man etched by sorrow and struggle, his life a tapestry of resilience and regret. His story began with an encounter in 1990, a singular, chilling event that would forever shape his destiny.

At the tender age of 19, Tony was no stranger to the rugged beauty of Cedarville's wilderness. Yet, one fateful day along the banks of the Wabash River, he survived an encounter that tore apart the fabric of his youthful innocence. It left him deeply scarred, a wound that time has failed to heal, a constant reminder of the past that he cannot escape.

The years that followed were marked by an attempt to find normalcy. Tony fell in love, and for a while, it seemed like he might escape the ghost of his past. He married a woman whose smile could light up the gloomiest of days, her laughter a balm for his wounded soul. Their love was profound, yet their home remained silent, devoid of the patter of little feet. They never had children, a void that added a tinge of melancholy to their shared existence. However, life had another cruel twist in store. His wife, his source of happiness, was diagnosed with breast cancer. Tony helplessly watched as the woman he loved withered away, her light dimming gradually until one day, it went out completely. His world collapsed, and the ghost of his haunting past returned, more potent than ever.

In his grief, Tony fled Indiana, hoping that distance would dull the pain, that new surroundings would help him forget. He tried to outrun his past, to escape the memories that clung to him like a second skin. Yet, the specter of his encounter in 1990 and the loss of his wife were constant companions in his solitude. Years passed until the death of his parents brought him back to Cedarville. He inherited the family home, a place echoing with memories of a simpler time, a time before his life was irrevocably altered. Living in his childhood home only emphasized his loneliness, each room a reminder of his solitude.

Despite the weight of his past, there's a kindness in Tony that life hasn't managed to extinguish. He is a good man, a gentle soul bearing the burden of his guilt and grief. He carries his sorrow with a quiet dignity, his loneliness a silent companion only interrupted by the occasional visitor or the soothing murmur of the nearby Wabash River. Each room in his inherited home whispers stories of his past - the laughter, the love, and the losses. The wallpaper, faded with time, holds onto the echoes of his mother's lullabies, while the wooden floorboards creak under the weight of his father's missed footsteps. The emptiness of the house mirrors his own - a vast expanse filled with echoes of what once was.

Tony's life is a testament to the human spirit's resilience. He is a man who has faced the unthinkable, yet continues to put one foot in front of the other. His heart, though scarred, still holds an abundance of love and kindness. His story is a poignant reminder that even in the face of despair, the human spirit can endure.

Haunted by his past and plagued by guilt, Tony's return to Cedarville was not easy.

However, it was the discovery of Bryan's podcast that stirred something within him. The recounting of Bryan's own encounter resonated with Tony's buried memories. This revelation led him to a crucial decision - it was time to confront his past.

The decision to unveil his secrets was not a light one. It meant reopening old wounds, reliving the terror of that fateful day in 1990. Yet, he recognized it as a necessary step toward healing, a chance to share his burden with someone who might understand.

As Tony steps forward to confront his past, he stands on the precipice of change. His journey of survival, love, loss, and loneliness has led him to this moment. He is a man haunted, a man scarred, but beneath it all, a man of incredible strength and kindness. His story is a testament to the enduring spirit of Cedarville, a town that, like Tony, bears the marks of its past with a quiet, resilient dignity.

Bryan adjusted the microphone in front of him, his heart pounding with anticipation. Today was the day he would welcome Tony, a guest whose encounter would shed light on the truth that had remained hidden for far too long. He took a deep breath and began recording.

Brandon Wright © 2023

"Welcome to *Beastly Encounters*, Tony. Thank you for joining us today. I'm glad to have you here with me, in person, for this interview tonight." Bryan greeted, his voice filled with a mix of excitement and reverence.

"Thanks for having me, Bryan. It's good to finally have a platform where I can share my story," Tony responded, his voice tinged with a sense of urgency.

Bryan leaned in, his curiosity piqued. "So, Tony, your story captivated me, being local to this area, I wanted to have you on here to share your experience. If you're ready, please tell us about that horrifying night in July of 1990. Take us back to the camping trip near the Wabash river and recount the events in as much detail as you can."

Tony's voice trembled slightly as he began, his words painting a vivid picture of the horrors that unfolded that fateful night.

"We had a group of five of us, all college buddies looking for a weekend getaway. The camping spot near the Wabash river seemed perfect, secluded and surrounded by nature. Little did we know the nightmare that awaited us," Tony began, the weight of his memories evident in his voice.

"We set up our tents, laughing and joking, completely unaware of anything that lurked nearby. As the sun began to set, we gathered around the campfire, sharing stories about girls and just enjoying the beauty of the night. But then, we heard it...a low growl in the distance, like nothing we had ever heard before. You could almost feel it reverberate through your body."

Bryan leaned closer to the microphone, captivated by Tony's words. "What happened next, Tony? Can you describe what you saw?"

Tony took a deep breath, his voice steady yet filled with dread. "It emerged from the tree line, its eyes glowing with an otherworldly intensity. It stood on two legs, towering over us, a grotesque combination of man and beast. Its fur was matted and dirty, its teeth sharp and glistening in the moonlight. We were frozen in terror as it approached, its heavy footsteps sending shivers down our spines."

Bryan's heart raced as he listened intently, the details of Tony's encounter sending chills down his spine. "And what did it do, Tony? How did it attack?"

Tony's voice quivered as he recounted the grisly details of the creature's attack. "It moved with unimaginable speed, tearing through our campsite as if it were made of tissue paper. The creature's claws sliced through the tents like hot knives through butter, leaving a trail of

Brandon Wright © 2023

shredded fabric in its wake. We were paralyzed with fear, unable to comprehend the sheer violence unfolding before our eyes. Mark, my dear friend, was the closest to the creature when it lunged at him. Its massive jaws clamped down on his shoulder, its teeth sinking deep into his flesh."

Tony's voice cracked with anguish as he continued, his words laced with sorrow. "We screamed in terror, desperately trying to free Mark from the creature's grip. But it was relentless, shaking him like a ragdoll, its strength overpowering. Blood sprayed through the air, staining the ground crimson as Mark's life force drained away."

Tears welled up in Bryan's eyes as he listened to the harrowing tale. The helplessness Tony must have felt, witnessing his friend's brutal demise, sent shivers down his spine. The weight of the unsung truth grew heavier with each passing word.

"We tried to fight back, throwing whatever we could find at the creature, but it seemed impervious to our attempts. It was a force of nature, fueled by an unimaginable rage. And then, just as suddenly as it had appeared, the creature vanished into the darkness, leaving us in a state of shock and devastation."

Silence hung heavy in the air as Tony's recounting of the attack came to an end. The weight of the unspeakable horror they had experienced settled upon them like a suffocating fog.

Bryan's voice trembled as he spoke, his empathy for Tony and the tragedy they had endured evident in his words. "I can't even begin to imagine the pain and horror you went through that night, Tony. To witness the loss of a friend in such a brutal manner... it's unimaginable. I'm so sorry."

Tony's voice was filled with a mix of grief and sincerity. "Thank you, Bryan. It's been thirty years, and the truth has been buried beneath a web of lies. Mark's death was written off as a bear attack, but bears don't behave like that. Something else was responsible, something far more sinister."

Bryan's resolve hardened as he listened, his desire to uncover the truth burning brighter than ever. "You're right, Tony. We owe it to Mark."

Bryan's mind raced as he absorbed Tony's words. The injustice of it all, the blatant cover-up and manipulation of the truth, was infuriating. The local government's involvement, the arrival of mysterious men in black suits, and the forced acceptance of the bear attack explanation left a bitter taste in his mouth.

"You know, Tony," Bryan said, his voice filled with anger. "The fact that bears don't even inhabit this part of Indiana only adds to the absurdity of their explanation. It's clear that something more sinister was at play that night."

Tony sighed, the weight of guilt evident in his voice. "After the agents arrived, everything changed. They took over the investigation, dismissing our accounts and ruling it as a mere bear attack. They warned us to keep quiet, to accept their version of events. And we, afraid of the consequences, went along with it."

A sense of anger surged within Bryan as he realized the extent of the deception. "Tony, you shouldn't blame yourself. You were coerced, manipulated into silence. It's not your fault."

Tony's voice trembled with a mix of shame and heartbreak. "I know, but it doesn't make it any easier to live with. I feel like I failed Mark and his family by never admitting the truth. They deserved to know what really happened."

"You were scared, Tony, and it's understandable. But now, after all these years, you have the opportunity to right that wrong,"

Bryan replied, his voice filled with compassion. "By sharing your story and seeking the truth, we can honor Mark's memory and ensure that justice is served."

A moment of silence passed between them as the weight of their shared mission settled upon their shoulders. The truth had been buried for far too long, and it was time to unveil the conspiracy that had shrouded their encounters.

Bryan leaned forward, the soft glow from the lamp casting a warm light on his earnest face. "Tony, what happened to the others?" he asked, his voice gentle, but firm. "The three survivors from that night in 1990?"

Tony shifted uncomfortably in his chair, his fingers nervously playing with the frayed edges of his shirt. His eyes, heavy with decades of regret and sorrow, met Bryan's. "After that night...we didn't speak of it again," he said in a low, gruff voice that barely disguised the pain he carried. "In all honesty, we didn't really talk to each other again."

Bryan remained silent, giving Tony space to gather his thoughts. He knew that he was treading on sensitive ground, navigating the painful memories that Tony had kept buried for so long.

"Greg...he didn't make it past a year," Tony continued, his voice trembling slightly. "Some said he...he did it himself. But I never really knew for sure." His voice trailed off and he looked away, the unsaid words hanging heavily in the air.

Bryan felt a pang of sympathy for Tony. The trauma from that horrifying night had clearly taken a toll on all of them.

"And Frank and Phil?" Bryan asked, his voice barely above a whisper.

"Frank moved away not long after," Tony said, a distant look in his eyes. "We lost touch. Haven't seen or heard from him since." He paused, taking a deep breath before he continued. "Phil...Phil passed away about twelve years ago. Had a heart attack while working on his farm."

The room fell silent, the only sound was the soft ticking of the clock on the wall. Bryan could see the toll the memory was taking on Tony. The haunted looks, the quiet remorse, the deep sadness. It was clear that the horrific event had not only claimed Mark's life but had also ended their friendships, carving a deep gulf of trauma and guilt between the survivors.

Bryan reached out, placing a comforting hand on Tony's. "I'm sorry, Tony," he said softly. "I can't imagine how hard it must have been for all of you."

Tony just nodded, his gaze fixed on the floor. The pain of the past was etched deep in his eyes, a stark reminder of the horror that had forever changed their lives.

"We can't let fear dictate our actions any longer," Tony declared, his voice filled with newfound determination. "We owe it to ourselves, to Mark, and to all those who have encountered these creatures to dig deeper, to unravel the web of lies and expose the truth."

Bryan's voice echoed with resolve as he responded, "You're right, Tony. We will investigate further, uncover every piece of evidence, and bring the truth to light. We won't rest until justice is served and the world knows what really happened that night."

With their shared beliefs as their guide, Bryan and Tony embarked on a mission that would hopefully inspire others to join the cause.

The next morning, Bryan and Tony set their plan into motion. They created a dedicated email address and a hotline for witnesses to come forward, ensuring their anonymity and safety. They also reached out to local newspapers, online forums, and social media platforms, spreading the message far and wide.

Their message was clear: If you have witnessed a similar encounter, if you have been told that these attacks were mere animal incidents, it is time to break the silence. Join us in the fight for truth, justice, and the recognition of the horrors that lurk in the shadows.

As the days passed, responses began pouring in. Witness after witness stepped forward, sharing their harrowing tales of encounters with the mysterious creatures. Their stories mirrored the details Tony had shared—the speed of the attacks, the ferocity of the creatures, and the subsequent cover-ups.

With each new account, Bryan and Tony's resolve strengthened. They realized they were not alone in their quest for truth. The movement they had begun was growing, fueled by the shared experiences of those who had been silenced for far too long.

The evidence they had gathered was compelling. Photographs of shredded tents and claw marks, audio recordings of bone-chilling howls in the dead of night, and even video footage of a creature lurking in the distance—all of it was presented on the *Beastly*

Encounters podcast, amplifying the voices of the witnesses and challenging the official narrative.

4   TROUBLE ABOUND

As the weeks went on, the tension in the air was palpable as Bryan and Laney stood in the middle of their living room, their voices raised in a heated argument. The weight of the recent events and the growing attention surrounding Bryan's pursuit of the truth had taken its toll on their family.

"Laney, I understand your concerns, but we can't let fear dictate our actions," Bryan pleaded, his voice filled with desperation. "People need to know the truth, and we can't turn our backs on those who have suffered."

Laney's eyes welled up with tears, her voice filled with frustration. "I'm not asking you to turn your back on anyone, Bryan. I just worry about the kids and the impact all of this is having on them. They're being teased at school, and it's not fair to them."

Bryan's heart sank as he realized the unintended consequences of his actions on his family. He had been so consumed with the pursuit of truth that he had neglected to consider the toll it was taking on his loved ones.

"You're right, Laney. I've been so focused on this mission that I've neglected our own well-being," Bryan admitted, his voice softened with remorse. "I never wanted our children to suffer because of my actions. I'll find a way to protect them while continuing to fight for justice."

Laney's expression softened as she saw the sincerity in Bryan's eyes. "I know you're passionate about this, babe. And I don't want to stand in the way of what you believe in. But we need to find a balance, a way to protect our family while you still pursue the truth."

Bryan nodded, sadness etched on his face. "You're right. We'll sit down together and come up with a plan to ensure our children's safety and well-being. They come first, always."

With their argument resolved, Bryan and Laney sat down together, their heads bent in deep conversation. They discussed ways to shield their children from the negative attention, to create a safe and nurturing environment for them amidst the chaos.

Meanwhile, Tony had been patiently waiting for Bryan's arrival to discuss the recent attack and their plan to investigate the area. He understood the strain it was putting on Bryan's family and respected the need for balance.

When Bryan emerged from the conversation with Laney, his face held a mix of determination and concern. "Tony, we need to investigate this recent attack, but we also need to ensure the safety of my family."

Tony understood, without hesitation, he nodded his head in agreement. "You got it, Bryan. We'll be careful."

As the sun began to set, casting long shadows across the landscape, Bryan and Tony headed towards a secluded spot near Whispering Pines State Park. The air was thick with anticipation and a sense of foreboding. Tony had devised a plan to investigate the recent attack, but the darkness that surrounded them seemed to amplify their fears.

Whispering Pines State Park, once a sacred land belonging to Native American tribes, holds a dark and twisted history that has plagued the area for decades. Locals speak in hushed whispers of the park's haunting presence, where eerie happenings and unexplained phenomena have become all too common.

For years, hikers have ventured into the depths of the woods, only to disappear without a trace. Their sudden vanishing leaves a chilling void, and the community anxiously awaits news of their fate. Official investigations often conclude these cases as wild animal or bear attacks, despite the absence of bears in Indiana. Yet, the gruesome aftermath and the stories whispered among locals paint a much more sinister picture.

Reports of animal attacks are not uncommon, but the savagery and brutality of these incidents surpass any known predator in the region. Witnesses recount horrifying encounters with creatures that defy logic and comprehension - twisted figures with glowing eyes and unearthly growls that stalk the woods with malevolent intent. These sightings have persisted over the years, leaving an indelible mark on the collective consciousness of the community.

The haunted history of Whispering Pines State Park traces back to its origins. Once a sacred and revered land, it held a deep spiritual significance for the Native American tribes that resided in the area. Legends speak of ancient curses cast upon the land, punishments for trespassing or desecrating the sacred grounds.

As time passed, the land was taken over, and the spiritual connection severed. The arrival of settlers and the encroachment of modern civilization disrupted the delicate balance that once existed. The spirits of the land, angered by the intrusion, unleashed their fury upon those who dared to set foot in their domain.

Over the years, attempts to investigate these strange occurrences have been met with resistance and skepticism. Authorities, under pressure to maintain order and preserve the reputation of the park, dismissed the claims as mere superstition or wild imagination. The truth, however, remains hidden beneath layers of deception and denial.

Whispering Pines State Park stands as a haunting reminder of the past, where ancient spirits hold sway and the curse of the land lingers. The restless souls of the Native American tribes who once called this place home continue to seek vengeance, their presence felt in the chilling winds that whisper through the pines. A testament to the resilience of legends, the power of curses, and the relentless pursuit of the unknown. It serves as a chilling backdrop to the lives of those who call Cedarville home, a constant reminder that there are forces beyond comprehension that lurk in the shadows, waiting for those who dare to venture too close.

`   "Bryan, I've been doing some research," Tony began, his voice filled with a mix of excitement. "There have been reports of similar attacks in nearby towns, going back decades. It's as if these creatures have been haunting our region for generations."

Bryan's eyes widened with both curiosity and unease. "So, you're saying that this isn't just a more recent phenomenon? That these attacks have been happening for years, and no one has spoken up? I know your encounter was 30 years ago, but I never thought it could be such an elaborate plan to conceal it for so long."

Tony nodded solemnly. "Exactly. It seems that the authorities have been covering up the truth for a long time, dismissing these incidents as mere animal attacks or accidents. But the evidence suggests otherwise."

A shiver ran down Bryan's spine as he listened to Tony's words. The darkness seemed to press in on them, enclosing them in a suffocating embrace. The suspense and dread in the air were almost tangible.

"We need to proceed with caution, Tony," Bryan whispered, his voice barely audible over the rustling leaves. "We don't know what we're up against, and if these creatures truly exist, we could be walking into a dangerous situation."

Bryan and Tony arrived at a small, remote mobile home in the woods, where Avery Williams had agreed to meet them. The tension in the air was palpable as they approached the door, ready to hear her account of the horrifying encounter.

Avery, a young woman of Native American descent, with haunted eyes, welcomed them inside. The room was bathed in soft candlelight, creating an atmosphere of both vulnerability and secrecy. She seemed on edge, her voice trembling as she recounted the events of that fateful night.

"I can still hear the sounds," Avery began, her voice barely above a whisper. "It was late, and we were sitting around the campfire. That's when I saw it — a massive creature, like a mix between a wolf and a man, lurking in the shadows."

Her hands trembled as she described the creature's glowing eyes and its chilling, inhuman growls. Bryan and Tony listened intently, their minds racing with questions and possibilities.

"What did it do?" Tony asked, his voice filled with a mix of curiosity and concern.

Avery took a deep breath, her eyes welling with tears. "It attacked," she replied, her voice filled with anguish. "It came out of nowhere, tearing into the tents and dragging those poor people away. The screams... I can still hear them, haunting my dreams."

Bryan's heart clenched at her words. The gravity of the situation sank in, and he knew they were dealing with something far more sinister than they had initially anticipated. The deaths were not random acts of violence but the result of a malevolent force lurking in the shadows.

"Do you have any idea why these creatures are targeting people?" Bryan asked, his voice tinged with both fear and curiosity.

Avery hesitated, her gaze darting around the room as if afraid of being overheard. "I've heard rumors," she whispered. "Whispers of ancient curses, of a connection to the land itself. Some say these creatures are guardians, protectors of something hidden deep within these woods."

Bryan and Tony exchanged glances, the weight of the revelation settling upon them. They had unknowingly stumbled upon a mystery far more complex and dangerous than they had imagined. The creatures were not merely mindless predators; they had a purpose, a deeper connection to the land.

As Avery's words hung in the air, a tense silence settled over the room. Bryan and Tony felt the weight of the revelation pressing down upon them, each lost in their own thoughts.

Bryan's mind raced, trying to piece together the fragments of information they had gathered. The idea that these creatures were more than mindless killers intrigued him. It hinted at a hidden history, a dark secret that had been concealed within the depths of these woods.

Tony, ever the skeptic, leaned forward and asked, his voice laced with doubt, "But why would these creatures choose to protect something by killing innocent people? It doesn't make sense."

Avery sighed, her eyes filled with a mix of fear and resignation. "I don't have all the answers," she admitted. "But there are whispers of sacrifice, of appeasing some ancient power. The people who have lost their lives, they might be seen as offerings to whatever these creatures serve."

The room grew even more suffocating, the weight of the knowledge threatening to drown them all. Bryan and Tony exchanged a glance, both realizing the enormity of the task before them. They had stumbled upon a dark secret, a dangerous truth that demanded their attention.

Determined to uncover the truth, Bryan spoke, his voice filled with resolve. "We can't let this continue. Innocent lives are at stake, and we have to find a way to stop these creatures, whatever it takes."

Tony nodded in agreement, his skepticism momentarily silenced by the gravity of the situation. "We'll need to gather more information," he said, his voice tinged with a mix of caution and determination. "We have to understand the history, the significance of this land. Only then can we hope to find a way to protect ourselves and others."

As they left Avery's home, the tension in the air remained, thick and suffocating. The weight of their newfound knowledge pressed down upon them, fueling their quest to uncover the truth and put an end to the terror that plagued these woods.

The journey ahead was uncertain, fraught with danger and unanswered questions. But Bryan and Tony knew that they had no choice but to push forward, to confront the darkness head-on. The fate of not only themselves but of those who had already fallen rested upon their shoulders.

With a renewed sense of purpose, they set out, their minds filled with a mix of fear and resilience. The path ahead would test their limits, but they were ready to face whatever horrors awaited them in their quest for answers and justice. The knowledge that innocent lives were at stake ignited their determination, pushing them to delve deeper into the dark secrets of the land.

5 ON THE HUNT

The days turned into weeks as Bryan and Tony tirelessly searched for clues, poring over ancient texts and speaking with locals who had lived in the area for generations. Each conversation, each piece of information, added to the growing tapestry of the mystery they were unraveling. They would continue to make trips to the woods, searching for any sort of evidence they could collect.

But with every step forward, the tension grew. They could sense the presence of the creatures lurking just beyond their reach, watching and waiting for an opportunity to strike. The forest seemed to close in around them, its once serene beauty now a shroud of darkness and danger.

As the clues and whispers began to align, a chilling realization dawned on them. The land they were investigating held a history steeped in ancient rituals and forgotten lore. It was a place where the boundaries between the natural and supernatural realms blurred, where the veil of reality thinned.

The tension hung heavy in the air as they took their first steps into the unknown. The fate of the forest, of innocent lives, rested on their shoulders. But they were resolute, driven by the weight of their mission that bore heavily upon them. The air grew thick with anticipation, each step bringing them closer to the confrontation that would determine the fate of the land.

Bryan and Tony parked their car at the edge of the forest, the headlights cutting through the darkness, casting long, eerie shadows on the surrounding trees. The atmosphere was heavy with a sense of foreboding, the news of a recent animal attack adding an extra layer of tension to their already nerve-wracking mission.

Bryan had received a tip from someone who reached out to the *Beastly Encounters* email. The tip gave coordinates to an area where a recent animal attack was currently under investigation.

Tony glanced at Bryan, his brow furrowed with concern. "Did you hear about the attack that happened here just a day or two ago? It's getting too close for comfort," he said, his voice laced with unease.

Bryan nodded, his eyes scanning the area. "Yeah, it's definitely unsettling. The frequency of these attacks is increasing, and it's not just wild animals. Something strange is happening here, Tony, and I think we're on the right track to finding answers."

They grabbed their equipment, ensuring they had everything they needed for their investigation. As they made their way into the darkened forest, their footsteps muffled by fallen leaves, the silence hung heavy between them. The occasional hoot of an owl or rustle of underbrush amplified the eeriness of their surroundings.

Tony swallowed hard, his voice breaking the silence. "You know, Bryan, I can't help but wonder if we're getting in over our heads. These woods... they have a reputation. People have gone missing here, and those who have returned, well, they're never the same."

Bryan shot him a reassuring look. "I understand your concerns, Tony, but we can't let fear hold us back. We've dedicated ourselves to uncovering the truth, shedding light on the unknown. If we let the legends and stories scare us away, we'll never find the answers we're looking for."

Tony nodded, a mixture of determination and unease in his eyes. "You're right. We can't let fear control our actions. We owe it to those who have vanished, to the community, to find out what's really going on here."

They pressed on, their flashlights piercing through the thick undergrowth, creating eerie shadows that danced on the trees. The air grew colder, a shiver running down their spines as they approached the area where the recent attack had occurred.

Bryan's voice was barely a whisper, filled with a mix of excitement and caution. "This is it, Tony. The place where it happened. We need to keep our senses sharp and be prepared for anything. Whatever is out there, we need to be ready."

Bryan glanced at his phone, with a couple of unanswered text messages from Laney being highlighted on the lock screen. They had ventured to an area where there was no cellular service, but Bryan could tell by the texts that his wife was concerned. Bryan turned to face Tony, his eyes filled with unease. "Tony, I need you to do something for me," he said, his voice steady but tinged with urgency.

Tony looked at him, concern etched on his face. "What is it, Bryan? What do you need me to do?"

"I need you to go back to the car and drive to my place," Bryan replied. "Let Laney know that everything will be okay and that I'll be back soon. She's worried, and I don't want her to be freaking out all night."

Tony hesitated for a moment, torn between his loyalty to Bryan and his concern for Laney. "Are you sure you want to do this alone, Bryan? It's getting dangerous out here, and having someone by your side could make a difference."

Bryan placed a hand on Tony's shoulder, his voice filled with gratitude. "I appreciate your concern, Tony, but this is something I have to do right now. I need to follow this lead and see where it takes me. I can't let fear hold me back, and I don't want you to worry about me. Focus on helping me with taking care of Laney, and I promise I'll be safe. Besides, I've got my machete and gun with me, so I'll be fine."

Tony nodded reluctantly, his worry evident in his eyes. "Okay, Bryan. I'll go and let Laney know what's going on. But promise me you'll be careful out there. You've apparently always had a knack for finding trouble."

Bryan chuckled, a faint smile playing on his lips. "Trouble seems to find me, doesn't it? But don't worry, I'll keep my wits about me. Just make sure Laney knows I'll be back soon."

With a pat on Tony's shoulder, Bryan watched as his friend turned and headed back towards the car. As Tony disappeared from sight, Bryan took a deep breath, steeling himself for the unknown that lay ahead.

Alone in the darkened forest, he felt a mixture of fear and excitement. The weight of the recent animal attacks and the whispers of supernatural occurrences hung heavy in the air, but Bryan knew that he couldn't turn back now. He had to face the shadows head-on and uncover the truth that lay hidden within Whispering Pines State Park. With his flashlight in hand, Bryan continued his journey, his steps resolute and his heart filled with a burning determination. The mysteries of the park awaited him, and he was determined to uncover the secrets that lay within its depths.

As he continued on, each step forward intensified the tension. Shadows danced between the ancient trees, whispers of the creatures' growls echoing through the stillness. Fear threatened to consume him, but he pushed it aside, his pursuit for answers unwavering.

Finally, he reached the heart of the forest, where the ground seemed to pulse with an otherworldly energy. A sense of foreboding settled over him, but he knew he had to press on. He couldn't let fear paralyze him now.

Summoning all his courage, Bryan spoke, his voice steady despite the adrenaline coursing through his veins. "I know what you seek," he said, his words filled with conviction.

As he was prepared to venture into the darkness, his steps cautious and measured, Bryan couldn't shake the nagging feeling of unease. He thought of Laney and their children, hoping that they would remain safe as he delved deeper into the unknown.

Meanwhile, back at Bryan's home, Laney couldn't shake the sense of dread that had settled in her heart. The silence of the empty house seemed to amplify the eerie atmosphere, and every creak and groan sent chills down her spine.

She glanced at the clock on the wall, realizing that Bryan and Tony had been gone for hours. Concern gnawed at her, and she fought the urge to call them and demand they return home. But she knew that their pursuit of truth was important to them, and she had faith in their abilities to navigate the dangers they faced.

Laney sighed and tried to distract herself from the growing unease. She busied herself with tidying up the living room, but her mind kept drifting back to the recent events and the toll it was taking on her family. She couldn't help but worry about the safety of her husband and the potential danger they were exposing themselves to.

Lost in her thoughts, Laney jumped at the sound of a knock on the front door. Her heart raced as she cautiously approached, peering through the peephole before opening it. Relief washed over her as she saw Tony standing on the porch, his face etched with weariness and concern.

"Tony, thank goodness you're back," Laney exclaimed, unable to hide the worry in her voice. "Where's Bryan? Is he okay?"

Tony's expression softened, and he stepped inside, closing the door behind him. "Bryan is fine, Laney. We're taking every precaution. But we need your help."

Brandon Wright © 2023

Laney's eyes widened, her concern deepening. "What do you mean? What happened out there?"

Tony took a deep breath before responding, his voice filled with a mix of apprehension and determination. "We found something, Laney. Evidence that these attacks are not just random acts of nature. There's a pattern, a method to the madness. We need to gather more information, and we need your support."

Laney's heart sank as she realized the gravity of the situation. Her husband and Tony were delving into a world of darkness and danger, and she had to decide whether to stand by their side or plead for their safety.

She looked into Tony's eyes, seeing the same conviction that mirrored Bryan's. She knew she couldn't stand in their way, not when their pursuit of truth meant so much to them. With a steady voice, she nodded and said, "I'm with you, Tony. We'll do whatever it takes to uncover the truth and keep our loved ones safe."

Tony's expression softened, gratitude shining in his eyes. "Thank you, Laney. We'll be careful, and we'll keep you informed of any developments. Together, we have a chance to bring an end to this nightmare."

6   DEAD ENDS

B ryan stood at the edge of the police tape, his eyes fixed on the area where the two gruesome killings had taken place. The scene had been cleaned up, leaving no trace of the horror that had unfolded here. But he knew that there was something more to discover, something that the authorities had missed.

His heart pounding with a mix of curiosity and trepidation, Bryan took a deep breath, summoning his resolve. He knew he shouldn't be here, that he was trespassing on a crime scene, but he couldn't let go of the nagging feeling that there was a vital clue waiting to be uncovered. Carefully, he ducked under the police tape, his footsteps light as he ventured into the cleared area. The tension in the air was palpable, as if the very essence of the place was still haunted by the dark events that had transpired.

Bryan's eyes scanned the surroundings, searching for any sign, any clue that could shed light on the mysterious killings. But the area was devoid of any substantial evidence. Frustration gnawed at him, but he refused to give up.

As he turned to leave, a rustling sound caught his attention. His heart skipped a beat, his senses on high alert. He froze, his eyes darting around, trying to locate the source of the noise.

A figure emerged from the shadows, causing Bryan's breath to catch in his throat. It was Tony, his face etched with concern and relief. "Bryan, what are you doing here?" he asked, his voice filled with a mix of worry and admonishment.

"I had to see for myself," Bryan replied, his voice tinged with frustration. "There has to be something here, something that can lead us to the truth. But it seems like we're at a dead end."

Tony stepped closer, his gaze softening. "We'll find another way, Bryan. We can't risk getting caught or compromising the investigation. Let's head back to the vehicle and get somewhere safe. We'll come up with a plan then."

Reluctantly, Bryan nodded, realizing the truth in Tony's words. He knew he had taken a risk, a risk that could have jeopardized their entire mission. With a heavy sigh, he turned away from the crime scene, his mind already racing with new ideas and possibilities.

As they made their way back to the vehicle, the tension in the air remained, but so did their determination. They knew that the answers lay just beyond their reach.

Bryan and Tony settled into the vehicle, the weight of their recent discoveries and the looming darkness suffusing the air. The engine hummed to life, but a heavy silence hung between them, punctuated only by the sound of their breathing.

Tony glanced at Bryan, concern etched deep into his features. "You took a risk back there, Bryan," he said softly. "I understand your drive to find answers, but we can't afford to make mistakes. We need to be careful."

Bryan nodded, a mix of guilt and gratitude washing over him. Tony had always been the voice of reason, the compassionate soul that held the team together. His unwavering loyalty had earned him a special place in everyone's hearts.

"I know, man," Bryan replied, his voice heavy with remorse. "I just couldn't shake the feeling that there was something more to discover. But you're right. We need to focus on our mission, on finding a way to stop this darkness from continuing to destroy innocent people."

Tony's eyes softened, his gaze filled with understanding. "We're in this together, Bryan," he said, his voice filled with an understanding determination. "We'll find a way to bring an end to this nightmare. We won't let the darkness win."

As the vehicle rumbled along the forest road, the weight of their words hung heavy in the air. They had faced numerous challenges together, their bond forged through shared experiences and unwavering trust. The thought of losing Tony, of losing that unwavering support, sent a shiver down Bryan's spine. They had only known each other for several weeks, and their age difference had a different dynamic, but it wasn't so much father and son, but a mutual respect.

Hours passed, and the sun began to dip below the horizon, casting long shadows across the landscape. The vehicle came to a halt, they had made the trek back to Bryan's home.

Laney's eyes lit up as she saw Bryan, her worry giving way to relief. She rushed towards him, enveloping him in a tight hug. "Thank goodness you're okay," she whispered, her voice filled with genuine concern.

Bryan returned the embrace, a warm smile gracing his lips. "I'm here, Laney," he murmured, his voice filled with reassurance. "I'll always be here for you."

The team gathered around, their camaraderie palpable. Laughter and banter filled the air, momentarily pushing back the darkness that loomed over them. In that moment, the bond between them felt unbreakable, their unity a beacon of hope in the face of adversity.

As the evening settled in, Tony found himself surrounded by Bryan and Laney's children, their eyes wide with curiosity and excitement. With a warm smile, he began to play with them, engaging in games and laughter that seemed to momentarily lift the heaviness that hung over their lives.

Bryan and Laney watched from a distance, their gazes filled with a mixture of awe and admiration. They had always been cautious around new people, their past experiences leaving them wary of opening up. But Tony was different. There was an inherent goodness in him, a genuine love and passion for wanting to help others.

"I don't understand how he can have such a positive impact on everyone he meets," Laney whispered to Bryan, her voice filled with a mixture of awe and curiosity. "It's like he carries a light within him that dispels the darkness."

Bryan nodded, his eyes fixed on Tony as he engaged with the children. "There's something special about him, babe," he replied, his voice filled with a hint of wonder. "He sees the good in people, even in the darkest of times. It's like he has this unwavering belief that we can make a difference, that we can bring light to even the bleakest of situations."

As the laughter of the children echoed through the air, Tony's voice drifted towards them, filled with genuine warmth and compassion. "You see, my friends," he said, his voice carrying a hint of wisdom. "There is so much goodness in this world, so much love and hope. We just have to hold onto it, nurture it, and let it guide us through the darkest of times."

Laney and Bryan exchanged a glance, their hearts swelling with an appreciation for the man who had quickly become an integral part of their lives. In a world seemingly overrun by darkness, Tony's presence was a beacon of light, a reminder that love and compassion could prevail.

"We are lucky to have him with us," Laney whispered, her voice filled with gratitude.

Bryan nodded, a determined glint in his eyes. "We'll protect them, babe," he vowed. "We'll do everything in our power to ensure that his light keeps shining, and we bring the truth out for everyone to witness."

As the evening wore on, the laughter and joy continued, wrapping around the team like a warm embrace. In the midst of their mission to save the land from darkness, they had found solace and strength in the presence of Tony, a man who had unknowingly touched their lives.

7   ANONYMOUS TIP

B ryan sat in his cluttered office at the construction site, his mind far from the blueprints and project plans that lay before him. He couldn't shake the nagging feeling that there was more to the dark history surrounding the state park than they had initially uncovered.

His fingers tapped restlessly on the desk as he scrolled through the articles and reports he had managed to dig up. Avery's words echoed in his mind, fueling his obsession to uncover the truth.

As he stared at the screen, his inbox refreshed, revealing a new message. The sender's address was a jumble of random letters and numbers, a clear attempt to conceal their true identity.

Curiosity overcoming caution, Bryan clicked on the email. The message was succinct, containing only a few cryptic words: "Meet me at the secluded cabin in Whispering Pines State Park next weekend. There is something you need to see. Use the coordinates listed below. I'll be waiting."

Brandon Wright © 2023

His heart quickened with a mixture of excitement and curiosity. Who could have sent this? And what could they possibly want to show him? Could this be some sort of a trap? Without hesitation, he reached for his phone and dialed Tony's number.

"Tony, you won't believe what just landed in my inbox," Bryan said, his voice brimming with anticipation. "I received an anonymous email, inviting us to a secluded cabin in Whispering Pines State Park. They claim there's something we need to see."

There was a momentary pause on the other end of the line, and then Tony's voice crackled through the receiver. "Are you serious, Bryan? This could be our chance to uncover the truth about Cedarville. Count me in. Let's dig into this, and when we have enough information, we should head to that cabin, but we need to proceed with extreme caution."

As the day came to an end, Bryan returned home to find Laney putting their children to bed. The weariness of the day clung to him, but he couldn't help but share his excitement with her.

Brandon Wright © 2023

"Laney, I think we're onto something," he said, his voice filled with a mixture of anticipation and excitement. "Tony and I are planning a trip to the hunting cabin near the state park. I believe there's more to this story than meets the eye."

Laney looked up, her eyes shining with a mix of concern and support. "Be careful, Bryan," she cautioned. "I trust your instincts, but you're walking into dangerous territory. Promise me you'll stay safe."

Bryan nodded, his gaze unwavering. "I promise, Laney. We'll take every precaution. But we can't let fear hold us back. We owe it to those who have suffered to uncover the truth."

As the next couple of day's went by, Bryan found himself immersed in his research on the Whispering Pines State Park. He spent long hours pouring over old documents and talking to locals who had any knowledge of the park's history. The weight of his responsibilities began to take its toll, and the stress started to seep into his interactions with Laney.

Each night, as Bryan sat down with Laney to discuss his findings, he couldn't help but feel the tension in the air. His frustration at the lack of progress and the overwhelming workload was palpable, causing their conversations to become strained at times.

"I don't understand why this is so difficult," Bryan sighed, running a hand through his hair. "I feel like I'm hitting dead ends at every turn. It's fucking frustrating. This stupid email has me so worked up. Something about it seems off, but we can't afford to not investigate it."

Laney listened to him, her eyes filled with concern. She knew how much this investigation meant to Bryan, but she also saw the toll it was taking on him. "Bryan, remember why you started this," she said gently, reaching out to touch his arm. "It's not just about finding the truth, it's about you bringing justice and closure to those who have suffered. You can't give up now. Even if I wanted you to, I know this is something you believe you have to do."

He nodded, the weariness etched on his face. "You're right, babe. You're always right. I just... I want to make a difference, but it feels like I'm constantly hitting roadblocks. I don't want to let everyone down. Sometimes I feel like we are chasing shadows. I begin to question if there's anything actually out there, or if we're all just crazy."

Laney's grip on his arm tightened, her voice filled with unwavering support. "You're not going to let anyone down, babe. You're doing everything you can, and that's what matters. We're in this together, remember? Crazy or not, I believe in you."

In that moment, Bryan realized how fortunate he was to have Laney by his side. She was his anchor, the one who reminded him of his purpose and gave him the strength to persevere. He leaned into her touch, finding solace in her unwavering support. She became his sounding board, offering him a fresh perspective and helping him find the motivation to keep going.

"I'm sorry for bringing all of this stress home," Bryan murmured, his voice laced with exhaustion. "Sometimes, it just feels like it's all too much."

Laney turned towards him, her eyes filled with understanding. "You don't have to apologize, Bryan," she said softly, reaching out to stroke his cheek. "You know how much I love you, don't you? Your burdens are mine too."

A small smile tugged at the corner of Bryan's lips as he gazed into Laney's eyes. He felt a surge of gratitude for her unwavering love and support, especially during the most challenging times. Her love and understanding were the beacons that guided him through the darkest moments of their journey.

"I don't know what I did to deserve you," Bryan whispered, his voice filled with sincerity.

Laney's fingers gently brushed against his cheek, her touch conveying a depth of love that words could not describe.

In that moment, the room seemed to be filled with an unspoken understanding. No matter the challenges they faced, they would face them hand in hand, drawing strength from their shared love and unwavering support for one another.

In the stillness of the night, they found refuge in each other's arms, knowing that no matter what lay ahead, their love would guide them through. They drifted off to sleep, their hearts intertwined, ready to face another day together, united in their pursuit of truth and justice.

8   THE CABIN

B ryan and Tony set out on their investigation of the cabin, their conversations filled with a mix of meaningful discussions and shared worries. As they drove along the winding road towards the remote location, they couldn't help but feel a sense of both anticipation and dread.

"I can't help but wonder what we might find at this cabin," Tony said, his voice filled with a mix of excitement and apprehension. "Do you think this person is trying to toy with us?"

Bryan glanced at Tony, his eyes reflecting a similar blend of emotions. "It's hard to say, but I can't shake the feeling that there's something significant waiting for us there," he replied. "We owe it to ourselves, and to the victims and their families, to uncover any leads that might bring justice and closure."

Their discussions grew deeper as they reflected on the details of the investigations, analyzing the evidence they had gathered so far. They shared theories, debated possibilities, and tried to imagine what might have happened in that cabin all those years ago.

As they drew closer, the tension in the air became palpable. The dense forest surrounding the area seemed to close in, casting long shadows that danced ominously on the road ahead. The fading daylight added to the eerie atmosphere, enhancing their sense of anticipation.

Yet, despite the growing unease, there was a flicker of hope within both Bryan and Tony. They were determined to unearth any clues that might shed light on the dark past, and meeting with this mysterious person may help with bringing justice to the victims and closure to their families.

With their hearts filled with a mix of worry and hope, Bryan and Tony continued their approach to the cabin, ready to uncover the secrets that lay within its walls. The stage was set for a chilling and suspenseful investigation, where the past would intertwine with the present, and the answers awaited them in the darkness that awaited them at the cabin.

As the night wore on, the sense of dread and suspense only deepened. Bryan and Tony ventured deeper into the heart of the state park, their senses heightened and their resolve unwavering. They knew that what they would uncover could change everything, for better or for worse. Little did they know that everything was about to change.

In the heart of the state park, the darkness seemed to thicken around Bryan and Tony. Their flashlights cut through the blackness, casting eerie shadows on the trees that surrounded them. Every crackle of a twig underfoot sent a shiver down their spines, their senses on high alert.

As they cautiously continued their hike, a faint rustling caught their attention. They exchanged a glance, their eyes filled with a mix of curiosity and trepidation. Following the sound, they soon stumbled upon a clearing bathed in moonlight, revealing a disturbing sight.

The mutilated remains of a deer lay strewn across the ground, its body torn apart with precision. The sight was gruesome, and the metallic scent of blood hung heavy in the air. Bryan and Tony exchanged a knowing look that this was no ordinary animal attack.

Suddenly, a series of strange noises pierced through the silence, causing both men to freeze in their tracks. Their hearts raced, and they exchanged worried glances. Could it be one of the creatures they encountered years ago?

Just as panic threatened to consume them, a figure emerged from the shadows, revealing itself to be Special Agent Deacon Scott. A handsome young man, with a football player build, his presence alone alleviated some of their fears, but they remained on guard, unsure of his intentions.

Agent Scott approached them, his eyes scanning the surroundings with a trained vigilance. "Evening, gentlemen," he greeted, his voice carrying a calm authority. "What brings you out here in the midst of all this tonight?"

Bryan and Tony exchanged a quick glance, weighing their options. They decided to tread carefully, not yet revealing the true purpose of their mission. Tony cleared his throat and replied, "We could ask you the same thing. You don't appear to be with the Department of Natural Resources."

Agent Scott chuckled, a glimmer of amusement in his eyes. "Touché, gentlemen. I'm Special Agent, Deacon Scott with the Federal Bureau of Investigation. I'm actually here investigating the recent supposed bear attacks in the area. Seems like the forest has become the hunting ground for more than just wildlife."

Bryan and Tony nodded, their apprehension easing slightly. "We've heard about those attacks," Bryan said cautiously. "It's a dangerous situation out here. Seems a bit strange though that an FBI agent is out here by himself."

Agent Scott nodded in agreement. "Indeed, it is. That's why it's important for everyone to exercise caution. My partner is waiting for my arrival soon. So, what are you two doing in this neck of the woods?" he asked, his tone laced with curiosity.

The men exchanged another glance, silently deciding to withhold the full truth for now. Tony hesitated before answering, "We're working on a private investigation. Can't reveal all the details just yet, but we're looking for some answers."

Agent Scott raised an eyebrow, his interest piqued. "Ah, the mysterious private investigation. Well, I won't pry just yet, but if our paths align, perhaps we could lend each other a hand. I'm heading up this way to a cabin where my partner has setup a recon center for our investigation into these recent bear attacks. You two are welcome to follow along, help keep each other safe. You never know what's lurking out here in the shadows."

Bryan and Tony nodded, appreciating the agent's willingness to collaborate. The forest remained shrouded in mystery, but with Agent

Scott by their side, they felt a glimmer of hope amidst the uncertainty.

As Agent Scott led Bryan and Tony through the dense woods, he couldn't help but question their motives. He turned to them, a playful smirk on his face, and raised an eyebrow.

"So, gentlemen, I'll ask again, what sort of private investigation brings two middle-aged men like yourselves out here in the woods at this time of night?" he asked, his tone laced with amusement.

Bryan exchanged a hesitant glance with Tony, unsure of how much to reveal to the agent. "Well, Agent Scott, we're actually investigating a cold case," he finally replied, his voice tinged with both caution and hesitation.

Agent Scott's smirk widened, his eyes flickering with curiosity. "A cold case, huh? Must be quite the mystery to bring you out here to a place known for bear attacks. You two sure must know how to have a thrilling adventure."

Tony chuckled nervously, feeling slightly self-conscious under the agent's teasing. "Well, it seemed like the perfect setting to uncover some long-lost clues. Plus, who doesn't love a little danger, right?"

Agent Scott chuckled, his amusement evident. "I can't argue with that. But just remember, the woods can be a treacherous place, especially at night. You never know what you might stumble upon."

Bryan and Tony nodded, their expressions a mix of determination and apprehension. They were well aware of the risks, but their desire for answers outweighed their concerns.

As they continued their trek through the darkened forest, Agent Scott's playful banter persisted, interspersed with occasional warnings about the dangers that lurked in the wilderness. It served as a reminder of the risks they were taking, but also as a lighthearted way to ease the tension that hung in the air.

Despite the agent's teasing, Bryan and Tony remained focused on their mission. The bear attack served as a stark reminder of the unpredictability of their surroundings, but they were determined to press forward, driven by a relentless pursuit of truth.

With each step, the weight of the woods and their purpose deepened, creating an intricate tapestry of suspense and anticipation. The darkness enveloped them, and as they ventured further into the unknown, they couldn't shake the feeling that they were on the verge of uncovering something truly significant. Little did they know that their encounter with Agent Scott and their journey through the forest would be just the beginning of a chilling and mysterious investigation, where the line between reality and myth would blur, and the true horrors of the past would slowly reveal themselves.

As Agent Scott continued leading Bryan and Tony through the thick foliage, he couldn't resist teasing them further. His playful banter became a constant presence, serving as both a source of amusement and a way to lighten the mood.

"So, gentlemen, how did two seasoned investigators like yourselves decide that hiking through the woods at night was going to help your cold case?" Agent Scott asked, a mischievous glint in his eyes.

Bryan chuckled, shaking his head. "Well, Agent Scott, sometimes you have to go where the evidence leads you, even if it means venturing into the wild."

Agent Scott nodded, a smirk playing on his lips. "Ah, the thrill of the chase. I can understand that. But just remember, if you encounter any bears, I suggest you don't try to interrogate them. They can be quite uncooperative."

Tony laughed, unable to resist the agent's humor. "Noted, Agent Scott. We'll keep our interrogation skills reserved for the human suspects."

The agent chuckled, his laughter echoing through the trees. "Good choice, Tony. I'm not sure how well bears respond to Miranda rights."

Their banter continued, providing moments of levity amidst the seriousness of their mission. Agent Scott's playful jabs and witty remarks helped to ease the tension, allowing them to momentarily forget the dangers that lurked in the shadows. As they walked deeper into the wilderness, the agent's comments turned more absurd, poking fun at their age and the situations they found themselves in.

"You know, fellas, they say wisdom comes with age," Agent Scott quipped, a twinkle in his eye. "But I'm not quite sure that applies to wandering around a forest looking for clues. I mean, what's next? Middle-aged men skydiving to solve a case?"

Bryan and Tony couldn't help but laugh, appreciating the agent's ability to find humor in the most unlikely situations.

"Who knows, Agent Scott," Bryan replied, a grin on his face. "Maybe we'll add skydiving to our investigative repertoire one day. Anything for justice, right?"

Agent Scott nodded, a smirk playing on his lips. "Now that's the spirit, gentlemen. I'd love to see you both in action, solving crimes while gracefully descending from the sky. That sounds like a heck of a movie, doesn't it?"

As they trekked through the wilderness, Agent Scott's banter began to touch on their investigative skills, gently mocking their approach.

"You know, Bryan, Tony, I've heard rumors that you two have a secret weapon in your detective arsenal," Agent Scott said, his voice filled with mock seriousness.

Curious, Tony raised an eyebrow. "Oh really? And what might that be, Agent Scott?"

The agent grinned mischievously. "Word on the street is that you've mastered the art of solving crimes by analyzing the patterns in squirrel behavior. Is that true?"

Bryan burst into laughter, unable to contain his amusement. "Well, Agent Scott, I hate to disappoint, but we haven't quite reached squirrel whisperer status yet. Our skills are more in the realm of logical deduction and careful analysis."

Agent Scott chuckled, shaking his head. "Ah, logical deduction, a classic detective's tool. But let's not underestimate the squirrels. They could be hiding vital clues up in those trees, you never know."

As the night grew darker and the sounds of the wilderness surrounded them, they couldn't help but appreciate the agent's ability to find humor in the most unexpected moments.

"You know," Agent Scott quipped, a twinkle in his eye, "I have to commend you both. Most people your age are content with a quiet evening at home, snuggling up to the old lady, but here you two are, in the middle of the fucking woods, chasing mysteries. It's impressive."

Tony chuckled, his steps growing more confident. "Well, Agent Scott, we like to think of ourselves as modern-day adventurers. Who needs a calm retirement when there are puzzles to solve?"

Agent Scott nodded, a smile tugging at the corners of his lips. "You have a point, Tony. Life is too short to sit on the sidelines."

Their banter echoed through the forest, intertwining with the rustling leaves and the distant hoot of an owl. It was a reminder that while their journey would be filled with challenges and unknowns. As they ventured deeper, Agent Scott began to reveal fragments of information, weaving a narrative that sent chills down their spines. He spoke of a secret government experiment, one that had gone awry years ago, unleashing a breed of creatures that were not quite animal, not quite human. These creatures had been responsible for the attacks, leaving a trail of bloodshed and terror in their wake.

Bryan and Tony listened in stunned silence, their minds struggling to comprehend the depth of the horror they were facing. It was not just a case of supernatural creatures; it was a conspiracy that reached the highest levels of power.

The path grew darker and more treacherous, the shadows seeming to dance menacingly around them. The suspense and dread were suffocating, threatening to overwhelm their resolve. But they pressed on, driven by a thirst for justice and a need to protect their loved ones.

Finally, they arrived at the secluded cabin, nestled deep within the woods. Bryan and Tony felt suspicious that Agent Scott was heading to the same location as they were supposed to be meeting with this mystery person, but they pressed on, determined to see what mysteries await. Its windows were boarded up, and the air hung heavy with an ominous silence. Agent Scott motioned for them to enter, cautioning them to be prepared for what they were about to see.

Inside, the room was filled with eerie artifacts and faded photographs. The walls were covered in notes and maps, each piece of evidence telling a story of unspeakable horror. It became clear that Agent Scott had been tirelessly investigating these attacks long before Bryan and Tony had stumbled upon the truth.

"Where's your partner, Agent Scott?" Bryan asked.

"Not here," Agent Scott replies, with a different demeanor about himself.

As the three of them poured over the evidence, a sudden crash echoed from outside, followed by a bone-chilling growl. The cabin shook violently, sending books and papers flying through the air. They were not alone.

Panic surged through their veins, their hearts pounding in their chests. The suspense and dread reached its peak as they braced themselves for the impending confrontation. With their weapons drawn, they ventured outside, the moonlight casting long shadows across the forest floor. Their eyes scanned the darkness, searching for any sign of movement.

And then, they saw them – the creatures, the ones they've seen before.

As Bryan and Tony stood in the clearing, the air seemed to crackle with a mixture of fear and anticipation. Agent Scott's voice broke the silence, revealing the chilling truth that lay beneath the surface.

"These creatures," Agent Scott began, his voice laced with a mixture of dread and awe, "they are not simply experiments gone wrong or interdimensional anomalies. They are the ancient gods, the beings that have haunted humanity throughout the ages."

Bryan and Tony exchanged a bewildered glance as the creatures' telepathic whispers echoed through their minds. The truth hit them like a tidal wave, leaving them stunned by the weight of centuries of myth and legend. Anubis, skinwalkers, werewolves - all manifestations of these creatures that had always dwelled among humanity.

Agent Scott continued, his voice filled with a grim determination. "These beings have the ability to traverse between our reality and theirs. They choose when to interact with us, when to feed on us. And now, they have decided it is feeding time."

As the gravity of the situation sank in, Bryan felt a knot tighten in his stomach. The safety of his family seemed even more precarious, and the urgency to escape this nightmare grew exponentially.

The creatures, sensing their vulnerability, surged forward, their monstrous forms closing in on Bryan and Tony. Fear pulsed through their veins, but Tony's love for his friend burned brighter than ever. With a final, resolute look, Tony made the decision that would change everything.

"Go, Bryan," Tony whispered, his voice tinged with heartbreaking resignation. "Get back to your family. I'll buy you time."

Tears welled in Bryan's eyes, his heart shattering as he watched Tony charge at the creatures, his weapon slashing through the air. The creatures descended upon him, their claws tearing into his flesh, their monstrous jaws closing around him in a brutal display of savagery.

Bryan's screams of anguish were drowned out by the sounds of Tony's valiant sacrifice. His friend's selflessness echoed through the trees, forever etching itself into Bryan's soul. With a heavy heart, Bryan turned and ran, his footsteps echoing through the night. The creatures pursued him, their hunger driving them with a relentless savagery.

But Agent Scott was not far behind, his footsteps matching the rhythm of the chase as Bryan sprinted through the darkness, his breath labored and his legs burning with exertion. Fear gripped him, but determination fueled his every step. He had witnessed Tony's sacrifice, his friend's life extinguished in the most brutal and heartbreaking manner. The weight of that loss propelled Bryan forward, refusing to let Tony's sacrifice be in vain.

The creatures' growls echoed behind him, their presence a constant reminder of the horror that pursued him. But even amidst the chaos, one voice stood out among the rest. Agent Scott's voice echoed through the night, taunting and sinister.

"You cannot escape, Bryan!" the agent's voice rang out, filled with malice. "You know too much. You must be silenced."

Bryan's heart pounded in his chest as the reality of the situation sank in. The agent, once a trusted figure, had orchestrated this entire nightmare, bringing Bryan and Tony to their deaths. He had used them as pawns in a twisted game, a game that Bryan now had to win in order to protect his family.

Pushing his exhaustion aside, Bryan veered off the main path, weaving through the underbrush in an attempt to lose his pursuers.

The forest seemed to conspire against him, branches clawing at his skin, roots threatening to trip him with every step. But he pressed on, driven by a desperate need to survive.

The creatures' snarls grew closer, their presence looming just behind him. Panic and despair threatened to overwhelm him, but he fought against it, channeling his grief and anger into a fierce determination.

Just when it seemed like all hope was lost, a glimmer of moonlight broke through the dense foliage. Bryan's heart leaped with a surge of hope as he realized he had stumbled upon a clearing. It was a small window of opportunity, a chance to gain some distance from his pursuers.

He sprinted towards the clearing, hoping that he could reach it before the creatures closed in. Adrenaline coursed through his veins, lending him a burst of speed. But just as he reached the edge of the clearing, a powerful force slammed into him from the side, sending him sprawling to the ground.

Agent Scott stood over him, a twisted smile on his face. "Game over, Bryan," he sneered, raising his weapon.

But before he could pull the trigger, a cacophony of snarls and growls filled the air. The creatures had caught up, their hunger driving them to attack. Without hesitation, Bryan slapped the gun out of his face, and delivered a kick to Agent Scott's right knee. This allowed Bryan to scrambled to his feet, pain shooting through his body as he darted away from Agent Scott and the encroaching creatures. He could hear their snarls behind him, the sounds of claws tearing through foliage, and the agonized cries of both man and beast intertwining in a macabre symphony.

Fear propelled him forward, his every instinct screaming at him to keep running. The moonlight guided his path, casting long shadows that danced around him, a haunting reminder of the horrors that lurked in the darkness.

As he sprinted through the undergrowth, a sharp pain seared through his leg, causing him to stumble. Glancing down, he saw blood oozing from a gash on his calf, evidence of the perilous chase he found himself in. With each agonizing step, the forest seemed to close in around him, its oppressive silence punctuated only by the occasional rustle of leaves or the distant howls of the creatures. Panic threatened to consume him, but he refused to succumb to despair. He had to keep going, for Tony, for his family, for himself.

For what felt like an eternity, Bryan wove through the labyrinth of trees, his breath ragged and his body pushed to its limits. But no matter how fast he ran, the relentless pursuit of the creatures never wavered.

Suddenly, a glimmer of hope pierced through the darkness. The distant sight of a dilapidated cabin emerged from the shadows, its weathered facade promising refuge from the horrors that pursued him. Without hesitation, he veered towards it, hoping that salvation awaited within its walls.

As Bryan burst through the cabin door, he found himself in a dark room, the air thick with the stale scent of abandonment. The sound of his own breathing echoed in his ears as he frantically searched for a means of escape or a weapon to defend himself. But before he could gather his bearings, a chilling presence filled the room. Agent Scott stood in the doorway, his eyes gleaming with a malevolent light. "You cannot hide, Bryan," he hissed, taking a step closer. "You will be devoured, like the rest."

A shiver ran down Bryan's spine, but he refused to let fear paralyze him. "You motherfucker!" Bryan yelled, with a surge of rage, he mustered every ounce of strength and lunged at Agent Scott, catching him off guard. The two grappled, their bodies crashing against the walls, furniture splintering through the chaos, Bryan fought with every fiber of his being. His fists collided with Agent Scott's face, his desperation fueling each blow. The agent's sinister grip tightened around Bryan's throat, cutting off his oxygen, but he refused to surrender. Summoning the last reserves of his strength, Bryan managed to break free from Agent Scott's grasp and stumbled backward. Gasping for air, he searched the room for anything that could aid him in this life-or-death struggle.

His eyes fell upon a dusty old fireplace, its iron poker resting against the hearth. Without a second thought, Bryan lunged for it, his fingers closing around the cool metal. He swung the poker with all his might, the force of his blow connecting with Agent Scott's arm, causing him to yelp in pain and release his hold. Seizing the opportunity, Bryan dashed towards the cabin's small window. He crashed through the decrepit glass, shards raining down around him. Blood trickled from his torn flesh, but he ignored the pain, propelled by the burning desire to survive.

Outside, the night air greeted him with a chilling embrace. The moon cast an ethereal glow on the surrounding forest, illuminating his path. He sprinted through the underbrush, the sounds of pursuit fading in the distance.

But just as he began to hope that he had eluded the creatures and Agent Scott, a low growl reverberated through the night. Glancing over his shoulder, Bryan's heart sank as he saw a pair of glowing eyes peering at him from the shadows.

The pursuit was far from over.

9 HIDE & SEEK

With the creatures once again on his trail, Bryan knew he couldn't afford to slow down. Terror and remorse mingled within him, urging him to keep pushing forward, to fight against the relentless forces that sought to consume him. As he ran, his mind raced, searching for a plan, an escape. He had to find a way to outsmart the creatures, to stay one step ahead of their predatory instincts.

The chase continued, Bryan stumbled onto the road, gasping for breath as he scanned his surroundings. The eerie silence sent shivers down his spine, but he pushed aside his fear and continued onwards, desperate to find any sign of civilization or safety.

As he caught his breath, a glimmer of hope sparked within him when he noticed headlights in the distance. He quickly realized it was a pickup truck approaching, and he waved his arms frantically, hoping the driver would see him and help. But his hope turned to despair as the truck swerved to avoid him, speeding past without stopping. Bryan's heart sank as he witnessed the horrifying scene that unfolded before his eyes. The creatures, drawn by the commotion, pounced on the vehicle, tearing through metal and glass with ease.

Their relentless hunger was unleashed as they overwhelmed the passengers, their screams of terror and pain piercing the night air. Bryan's gut twisted in horror, knowing that he was helpless to save them.

Filled with a mix of grief and terror, Bryan's survival instincts kicked in, urging him to flee from the macabre scene. He took off down the road, his legs pumping with adrenaline as the creatures were momentarily distracted by their gruesome feast.

Every step felt like an eternity as despair threatened to consume him. The weight of the world seemed to press upon his shoulders, but he refused to succumb to hopelessness. He had to keep running, had to find a way to survive.

As he sprinted, his eyes caught sight of a flickering light in the distance. It was a small farmhouse, standing defiantly against the encroaching darkness. With renewed determination, Bryan charged towards it, hoping that it would offer some refuge from the horrors that pursued him. As he neared the farmhouse, he could see the worn paint peeling from the weathered walls, a testament to the passage of time.

Bryan's heart pounded like a war drum as he sprinted towards the farmhouse, its pale silhouette a beacon of hope piercing through the black night. His lungs burned with each panicked breath and his pleas for help rang out, swallowed by the vast expanse of farmland.

"Let me in!" Bryan pounded on the door, the force shaking the old wooden frame. "Please, you've got to help me!"

The door creaked open, revealing an elderly couple bathed in the soft, warm glow of the house. The man, his face crisscrossed with deep-set wrinkles, held a shotgun with a steady hand that belied his age. His eyes held a wariness that turned to suspicion as he took in Bryan's disheveled appearance. They backed Bryan off the porch with the shotgun raised to his face.

"There are creatures out there!" Bryan gasped, his words tumbling out in a frantic rush. "They attacked me and my friend, and some people down on the road, and they've chased me here. You have to let me in! I'm begging you!"

The elderly woman, her frail body dwarfed by her husband's, shot a worried glance at Bryan, but the man remained unmoved. "You've been drinking, son," he grumbled, his voice as gravelly as the dirt road leading to the farmhouse. "We ain't entertaining your wild tales. Go sober up and leave our property."

Bryan's pleas grew desperate. "Please, you don't understand!"

His words cut off as a chilling howl tore through the night, followed by the guttural snarls of the creatures. Their eyes, glowing like embers in the darkness, locked onto the porch.

In an instant that seemed to stretch into an eternity, the creatures lunged. The couple had no time to react as the beasts descended upon them. A blood-curdling scream pierced the air, abruptly cut off as the creatures tore into their victims with a savagery that made Bryan's blood run cold.

With a surge of adrenaline, Bryan leapt into the house, his hand slipping on the doorknob as he slammed the door shut. He could hear the sickening sounds of the brutal attack outside, the frenzied snarls of the creatures and the final cries of the couple.

The lights flickered ominously before dying out, plunging Bryan into a terrifying darkness. He groped his way through the unfamiliar house, every shadow a potential threat. His heart pounded in his chest as he scrambled to find a hiding spot, the gruesome images of the attack playing over and over in his mind.

The terrifying sounds of the creatures echoed through the house, their growls vibrating the walls and sending icy tendrils of fear snaking up Bryan's spine. He could hear them scratching at the door, their guttural snarls filling the air.

Bryan stumbled into what felt like a small closet, the smell of mothballs and old coats filling his nostrils. He pushed his way past the hanging clothes, pressing himself into the darkest corner, praying he was hidden enough.

Outside, the creatures continued their frenzied assault on the door. The wood creaked under the relentless attack, each splintering sound a chilling reminder of the gruesome fate that awaited him if the door gave way.

Bryan could hardly breathe, his heart pounding so loudly he was certain the creatures could hear it. He clamped a hand over his mouth, stifling the terrified sobs that threatened to escape.

The attack seemed to go on forever, the creatures' savage snarls and the splintering wood the only sound in the otherwise silent house. Then, as suddenly as it had started, the assault stopped. The abrupt silence was somehow more terrifying than the attack. With trembling hands, Bryan pulled out his phone, desperately dialing Laney's number. Each ring felt like an eternity, his heart pounding in his chest as he waited for her to answer.

Finally, a quivering voice filled the line. "Bryan? Is that you?" Laney's voice was thick with tears, a mix of relief and anguish.

Shallow breaths escaped Bryan's lips as he fought back his own emotions. "Yes babe, it's me," he choked out, his voice filled with a mix of sorrow and love. "I need you to listen to me, please."

Laney's sobs intensified, the weight of the situation crashing down on her. "Oh God, Bryan, where are you? I'll call the police, I'll do anything, just tell me where you are!"

Tears streamed down Bryan's face as he heard the desperation in Laney's voice. He wanted nothing more than to hold her, to comfort her, but he knew the danger it would put her in.

"No, Laney," he forced the words out, his voice breaking. "I can't let anyone else come here. It's not safe, I've seen what they can do."

Laney's cries turned into pleas, her voice filled with a mix of fear and love. "Bryan, please, I can't lose you! We need you, I need you, the kids need you. Please, just tell me where you are so I can help!"

Bryan's heart shattered at her words, his guilt weighing heavily upon him. He had caused so much pain, so much despair, and he couldn't bear to put them at further risk.

"I'm so sorry, babe," he whispered, his voice filled with regret. "I need you to know that I love you, and I love our children more than anything. You made me so happy, and I'm sorry for everything."

Silence hung between them, broken only by Laney's muffled sobs. Bryan could picture her, clutching the phone tightly, her heart breaking with each passing moment.

"Bryan, please," she pleaded, her voice barely audible. "I can't lose you. We can find a way, we can fight this together. Just tell me where you are, please."

His heart ached, torn between his love for his family and his desire to protect them. "Laney, I can't risk it. I can't let anyone else get hurt because of me. Just know that I love you, and I'll always be with you, even if I can't be physically there."

Bryan's voice cracked with the weight of his emotions, his words barely audible over the sound of Laney's anguished cries on the other end of the line. The realization that this might be their final conversation tore at his soul.

"I'm so sorry, Laney," he repeated, his voice filled with despair. "I never wanted any of this to happen. Please, take care of our children, keep them safe. Tell them... tell them how much I love them."

Laney's choked sobs echoed through the phone, a symphony of heartbreak. "Bryan, please, there has to be something we can do. I can't bear the thought of a life without you."

His voice heavy with resignation, Bryan whispered, "I wish things were different. I wish I could be there with you, holding you, reassuring you. But this is the fucking reality I've made, and I can't change it."

Silence enveloped them once more, the weight of their shared grief hanging heavily in the air. The sound of Laney's ragged breathing was a painful reminder of the distance between them, of the impossibility of their reunion.

"Promise me, Laney," Bryan pleaded, his voice barely above a whisper. "Promise me that you'll keep our children safe, that you'll find a way to move forward without me. Promise me you'll remember the love we shared."

Laney's voice trembled as she responded, her words choked with tears. "I promise, Bryan. I'll protect them with everything I have. Our love will never be forgotten."

With a heavy heart, Bryan whispered his final words. "I love you, Laney. Always remember that. Stay strong for our children. Goodbye."

As he ended the call, the weight of his decision settled upon him. He was alone once more, consumed by the darkness that surrounded him. The creatures lurked in the shadows, their insatiable hunger closing in. A deep sense of hopelessness washed over Bryan, threatening to engulf him entirely. But a flicker of hope remained, a small flame that refused to be extinguished. In the face of despair, he would fight to survive, for himself, for his family, and for the love that would endure, even in the darkest of times.

As Bryan's heart pounded in his chest, he strained to distinguish the sounds outside. The noises grew louder, resembling the guttural growls and scraping claws of the Dogmen creatures he had encountered before. Accepting his fate, he resigned himself to the inevitable.

In a moment of desperation, Bryan clasped his hands together, closing his eyes tightly, and began to pray. It was a foreign act for him, someone who had never been religious, but in this moment, he was willing to try anything for a sliver of hope.

"Please," he whispered, his voice trembling. "If there's anyone out there listening, help me. Save me from these creatures. I don't want to die like this."

And then, to his astonishment, he heard a response. The same haunting voices he had heard earlier in his mind echoed back to him, their tone filled with a strange mixture of familiarity and otherworldliness. The creatures were outside, but they were asking him to "Let them in."

Confusion washed over Bryan. Why would they be asking for entry? Did they want to torture him further? He refused, his anger and confusion boiling to the surface. "Get out of my fucking head!" he shouted, his voice raw with defiance. "Leave me the hell alone!"

But the voice persisted, a chilling reminder of the enigmatic nature of his situation. "When you start to look into certain things, you should be worried about what is looking back," it whispered ominously.

Bryan's mind raced, trying to make sense of the cryptic message. What had he stumbled upon? What had he unknowingly invited into his life? Fear and anger mingled within him, fueling his determination to find answers, to survive and protect his family.

As the creatures continued their relentless pursuit, Bryan's resolve hardened. He would not succumb to their torment. With a newfound resilience, he gathered his strength, ready to face the unknown forces that were converging upon him. In the face of this bewildering and terrifying situation, Bryan's only choice was to push forward, to fight against the darkness that threatened to consume him. With each step, he would strive to uncover the truth, to protect his loved ones, and to confront the malevolent forces that had set their sights on him.

Bryan's heart raced as he swung open the door, his anger and defiance on full display. He stood there, facing the creatures head-on, unafraid and ready for whatever they had in store for him. "If you're going to attack me, then fucking do it, you bastards!" he shouted, his voice laced with a mixture of anger and desperation. "I hope you fucking choke on me!"

To his surprise, the creatures seemed to revel in his defiance. Their canine-shaped heads twisted into a sinister, unsettling smile. They bared their teeth, but instead of lunging at him, they crouched down and began to walk away.

Bewildered, Bryan watched as the creatures moved further into the darkness. He couldn't comprehend why they had chosen to spare him, but he wasn't about to chase after them. As they reached a distance, a strange flash engulfed them, and they vanished into thin air.

Confusion and relief washed over Bryan as he stood, the silence of the night settling around him. He couldn't shake the feeling that they might return, but for now, there was a momentary respite.

However, his newfound peace was shattered by the sound of a vehicle approaching in the distance. Panic surged through him as he realized his wife, Laney, had found him. He raced towards the road, torn between relief and concern for her safety.

As the vehicle drew closer, Bryan's heart pounded in his chest. He recognized his wife behind the wheel, her face etched with worry and fear. She had used the location tracking on his phone to find him.

Horrified that she had come here, he yelled at her, desperately urging her to leave. "We need to get out of here!" he exclaimed, his voice laced with a mixture of anger and relief. "It's not safe!"

But Laney, her eyes filled with tears, asked about Tony. The weight of his friend's death crashed over Bryan, and he broke down, his tears mingling with his words. "He's gone, Laney. Tony is gone," he choked out, his voice trembling with grief.

Without hesitation, Laney pulled him into her embrace, their tears intermingling as they clung to each other. They knew they couldn't stay in this place of darkness any longer. In a frenzy, they raced down the road, leaving the horrors behind them.

The creatures never reappeared, and as they drove further away, a glimmer of hope began to flicker within them. They clung to that hope, determined to find a way to move forward and rebuild their lives.

As they drove, the weight of his recent experiences settled heavily upon him. The horrors he witnessed, the desperation and hopelessness that had consumed him, were etched into their souls.

As they drove towards the horizon, a glimmer of hope ignited within them. They would find a way to protect their family, to protect other innocent people, and to expose the truth about the creatures. The desolation and despair that had threatened to consume them would not define their future.

Bryan and Laney held tightly to each other's hands, their grip a symbol of their unwavering commitment. They knew what they needed to do, but would anyone take Bryan's story seriously? Together, they would navigate the treacherous path ahead, guided by their strength and resilience.

10 IT'S ALL IN YOUR HEAD

As Laney guided Bryan towards the police station, her mind raced with worry. She knew that they needed to alert the authorities about the attacks and try to find some help. However, she couldn't help but feel a sense of unease as they entered the police station.

Bryan approached the officers at the front desk, his voice urgent as he tried to explain the terrifying events that had unfolded in the woods. "Officers, you have to listen to me. People are being attacked by some kind of creatures in the woods. We need your help."

The officers exchanged skeptical glances, their brows furrowing with suspicion. One of them, Officer Edwards, crossed his arms and leaned forward. "And what evidence do you have to support these claims, sir?"

Bryan's hands shook with a mixture of fear and frustration. "I don't have physical evidence, but there are witnesses, people who have been injured. We need to act quickly before more lives are at risk."

As Bryan spoke, more officers gathered around, their eyes fixed on him with increasing suspicion. The room grew tense, and Laney could feel the weight of doubt hanging in the air.

Just as the officers seemed ready to dismiss Bryan's plea, a voice called out from the entrance of the police station. "Hold on a moment."

All eyes turned towards the voice, and Bryan's heart skipped a beat when he saw Agent Scott standing there. He looked disheveled, his clothes torn, and his face marked with scratches.

Officer Edwards's eyes narrowed as he recognized Agent Scott. "Agent Scott? What are you doing here?"

Agent Scott approached with a determined expression. "Officer Edwards, I encountered this man in the woods. He's dangerous. He's the one responsible for the attacks."

The officers gasped, their suspicion turning into alarm. They took a step back, eyeing Bryan warily. Officer Edwards's voice hardened as he addressed Bryan. "Is this true? Are you responsible for these attacks?"

Bryan's eyes widened in disbelief and shock. "No, Officer, I swear I'm not responsible. He's the one causing all of this! I've been trying to survive, just like everyone else. Agent Scott is lying. It's him!"

Laney stepped forward, her voice trembling with urgency. "Officer, please, you have to believe us. Bryan saw the creatures, and he has been trying to protect people. We need your help."

The officers exchanged glances, torn between the conflicting testimonies. Officer Edwards's expression remained stern, but a flicker of doubt crossed.

As Laney stood beside Bryan in the police station, disappointment and frustration washed over her. The officers had listened to their pleas, but their skepticism had won out. Officer Edwards's voice was filled with doubt as he addressed Bryan.

"Sir, we appreciate your concern, but without concrete evidence or witnesses, we can't simply take your word for it. We will, however, launch an investigation into these alleged attacks. For now, we'll need to place you into custody until we gather more information."

Bryan's face contorted with a mix of anger and disbelief. "You can't be serious! I'm trying to save lives here, and you're treating me like a criminal? You have to believe me!"

Officer Edwards's expression remained stern. "We have a conflicting account from Agent Scott, who claims you attacked him. We must consider all possibilities. We will do our due diligence in this investigation, but until then, you'll have to cooperate with us."

Bryan turned to Laney, his eyes filled with determination. "Laney, this isn't over. You need to go home to the kids and keep them safe. We'll figure this out, I promise."

Laney's heart sank, torn between staying by Bryan's side and ensuring the safety of their children. Reluctantly, she nodded, knowing that she had to prioritize their well-being. "Alright, Bryan. I'll go home and make sure the kids are safe. I promise we'll find a way to clear your name."

Bryan took a deep breath, trying to hide the worry in his eyes. "Thank you, babe. Stay strong, and remember, I love you and the kids. We'll get through this."

As Laney left the police station, her mind was filled with a mix of fear and hopelessness. She knew she had to uncover the truth and find a way to prove Bryan's innocence. With a heavy heart, she returned home to their children, promising herself that she wouldn't rest until justice was served and their family was reunited.

Meanwhile, Bryan was escorted to a holding cell, his mind racing with frustration and anger. He knew he needed to find a way to clear his name, but it wouldn't be easy. Taking a deep breath, he prepared himself for the challenges that lay ahead, vowing to fight for justice and protect the town from the true threat that lurked within.

As Bryan sat alone in his cold, dimly lit cell, the voice of the creatures echoed in his head once more. Their words twisted and slithered, promising him freedom in exchange for his allegiance. But Bryan knew better than to make a deal with the unknown.

"I will never serve you," he whispered defiantly, his voice filled with determination. "I will find a way to expose the truth and clear my name, without your help."

The creatures' voice grew fainter, their hissing rage barely audible. Bryan could feel their anger and frustration, but he remained resolute. He knew that accepting their offer would only lead to more chaos and suffering.

With his mind set on uncovering the truth, Bryan began to devise a plan. He would use every resource available to him, leverage any connection he had, to gather the evidence needed to prove his innocence. He would not rest until justice was served and the true culprits behind the attacks were exposed.

As Bryan sat sulking, his mind filled with anger and confusion, he felt a sudden surge of telepathic communication. The voice was not his own, but that of Agent Scott, reverberating in his mind.

"Let me in, Bryan. Embrace the truth that lies within," Agent Scott's words echoed, laden with an eerie power that mirrored the communication of the supernatural beings.

Bryan's eyes widened, his heart pounding in his chest. The revelation shook him to his core. Agent Scott, the man he had once trusted, had made a deal with these creatures, willingly serving them in exchange for immortality. He had become their pawn, their conduit in the human world.

A mixture of fear and defiance swirled within Bryan's mind. He had witnessed the devastation caused by these entities, the lives they had taken. He couldn't fathom willingly becoming a vessel for their darkness.

"No, Scott. I won't let you in," Bryan replied, his thoughts resolute. "I refuse to become a goddamn puppet like you. There must be a way to stop them, to break free from their grasp."

Agent Scott's voice grew more insistent, tinged with a touch of desperation. "You don't understand, Bryan. They offer power beyond your wildest dreams. Immortality, control, everything you could ever desire. Embrace them, and together, we can rule."

Bryan's grip on his own identity tightened. He couldn't allow himself to be swayed by false promises and the allure of power. He had seen the destruction these creatures brought, the lives they had torn apart. He couldn't let their darkness consume him.

"I will never fucking join you, Scott," Bryan declared, his voice filled with defiance. "I won't become a pawn in their game. There has to be another way, a way to stop them without surrendering my humanity."

Agent Scott's thoughts sliced through Bryan's mind like a cold, sharp blade, his telepathic voice echoing in the stark emptiness of the holding cell.

"Oh, Bryan," Scott's voice held a cruel amusement. "You and Tony, you were so easy to manipulate. So eager to believe."

Bryan froze, his blood turning to ice in his veins. "What are you talking about?"

"The anonymous email? That was me, Bryan," Scott's thoughts were like venom, slowly spreading through Bryan's consciousness. "I led you right into my trap."

Anger, pure and seething, surged through Bryan. "You- you did this?" he spat out. His voice echoed in the empty cell, painting a vivid picture of a man unhinged to the police officers monitoring him from outside. To them, it appeared Bryan was arguing with himself.

"Yes, Bryan. I orchestrated it all. Tony's death? That's on you," Scott's voice was cold, unyielding. "You brought him there. You led him to his death."

The accusation hit Bryan like a punch to the gut. The walls of the cell seemed to close in on him as the gravity of Scott's words sank in. An overwhelming mix of guilt, grief, and rage washed over him. "You monster," Bryan's voice trembled with the force of his emotions. "You used us."

"All's fair, Bryan," Scott's voice was dripping with smug satisfaction. "It's survival of the fittest out here. Unfortunately, Tony just wasn't fit enough."

Bryan's rage was a physical entity, filling the cell with its intensity. "I won't let you get away with this, Scott," he vowed, his voice echoing against the cold, hard walls. "I will expose you."

Outside the cell, the police officers exchanged worried glances. To them, Bryan's heated argument with an invisible enemy only reinforced the notion of his madness. Little did they know; the true madness lay in the reality Bryan was forced to confront.

Agent Scott's voice faded, replaced by a chilling silence. Bryan sat alone in the cell, his resolve unwavering. He knew the road ahead would be treacherous, but he was determined to find a way to expose the truth, to free himself and others from the clutches of these malevolent beings.

In the holding cell, Bryan's mind raced with thoughts of his wife and children, the life he cherished. He couldn't bear the thought of leaving them behind, but he also couldn't allow the entities to manipulate him into becoming a monster. He was caught between two unfathomable choices, both leading to heartache and despair.

As the hours set in, Bryan sat alone in his cold, desolate cell, the weight of his choices bore down on him. The room was devoid of light, except for a dim glow filtering in through the small window. He could hear the distant sounds of footsteps echoing through the corridor, each one filling him with a mix of fear and anticipation.

Time seemed to stretch on endlessly as he waited, his mind filled with thoughts of his wife and children. Were they safe? Had they managed to escape the clutches of the creatures that haunted Cedarville? The uncertainty gnawed at him, a constant reminder of the consequences of his actions.

Suddenly, a knock on his cell door shattered the silence, causing Bryan's heart to skip a beat. His breath caught in his throat as he looked towards the door, his eyes wide with a mix of hope and caution. The cell door creaked open, and Detectives Johnson and Ramirez arrived at the holding cell where Bryan sat, the stark fluorescent lighting casting harsh shadows on his face. His eyes had a haunted look, reflecting the horrors he had witnessed.

"Bryan," Detective Ramirez began, her voice steady. She held a file in her hands, flipping it open to reveal several gruesome crime scene photos. "We need to talk about what happened."

Detective Johnson leaned against the cold bars of the cell, his gaze never leaving Bryan. "We found the bodies, Bryan," he said, his voice gravelly and serious. "Ronald and Doris Wilson, savagely murdered in front of their farmhouse. Your wife found you there, hiding."

Bryan's heart clenched at the mention of the elderly couple. He could still see their terrified faces, still hear their screams.

Detective Ramirez continued, her tone professional. "Further down the road, we found Jim Newson's truck. His body, along with his two young children, Aiden and Aurora, were scattered on the roadside. It looked like a wild animal attack...or something worse."

A lump formed in Bryan's throat. He remembered the children's screams, forever etched in his mind. He felt a cold shiver run down his spine. He could faintly recall the sound of a truck horn, the crunch of metal, and the screams, but it was all a blur now.

"And we found pieces of what we believe to be Mr. Baker near the cabin," Detective Johnson added, his voice barely more than a whisper.

Tears welled up in Bryan's eyes as he thought of his friend. He desperately tried to remember what had happened at the cabin, but his memories were hazy, fragmented. He kept seeing the creatures attack, and Agent Scott's laughter.

"There's more," Detective Ramirez continued, opening the folder to reveal a printed email. "It's a statement from Agent Scott. He was investigating recent animal attacks that he believed could be the work of a serial killer. He thought the killer was trying to make them look like animal attacks."

Bryan felt a knot form in his stomach. His obsession with the creatures of Cedarville had led him to cross paths with Agent Scott, but he had never imagined their paths would intertwine so horrifically.

"Scott was aware of your and Mr. Baker's involvement in the investigation," Detective Johnson said, his gaze boring into Bryan. "It piqued his curiosity. He sent you an email asking you to meet him at the cabin."

The memory of the email and their meeting at the cabin hit Bryan like a punch to the gut. He remembered the tension, the fear, but everything after was turning into blur.

"According to Scott, you had a mental breakdown at the cabin," Detective Ramirez said, her voice heavy with accusation. "He says you attacked and killed Mr. Baker. And when he tried to subdue you, you attempted to murder him too."

Bryan could hardly believe what he was hearing. Could he really have done such horrific things? Could he have become the monster he had been hunting? He knew these creatures exist, and he saw what they did. How could they try to blame him for such heinous crimes?

"And the people in the truck," Detective Johnson added, his voice grating on Bryan's nerves, "they were just bystanders, innocent people who stopped because they thought you needed help. And you...you murdered them too.

Like some sort of sick monster. They were children..."

Bryan's heart pounded in his chest. It wasn't true. He hadn't done these things. He was sure of it. But as the detectives laid out the evidence, Bryan began to question himself. Could he have done this? No, it was the creatures. They were real. He had seen them. They were the killers. But why was Scott framing him?

He looked up at the detectives, his voice barely a whisper. "It's a cover-up," he said, his voice shaking. "I didn't do this. You have to believe me."

The detectives exchanged a glance, their faces unreadable. Had he become the very monster he was hunting? Or was he the victim of a chilling conspiracy?

His mind flashed back to the gruesome scenes, the savage attacks, the terrified faces of the victims. The memory of the creatures, their glowing eyes and guttural snarls, was vivid and terrifying. But so was the image of Scott, pointing his gun at him, accusing him.

Bryan felt a cold dread seep into his bones. The evidence was damning, but he knew the truth. Or at least, he thought he did. The lines between reality and nightmare blurred, casting doubt on his sanity.

He replayed the events over and over in his head, each time adding more confusion. With each passing moment, Bryan felt himself sinking deeper into a pit of despair, the walls of his cell closing in on him.

His eyes fell on the cold, hard bench of his cell. It was a chilling reminder of his situation, of the accusations against him. Bryan lay down, his mind still a whirlwind of thoughts and fears.

The detectives' words echoed in his mind, their implications horrifying. Bryan felt a lump in his throat, a sense of dread settling in. He was trapped in a nightmare, and he didn't know how to wake up.

A heavy silence hung in the air as Bryan processed the words. The horror of what he was being accused of was too much to bear. He felt his sanity unraveling, the line between his obsession and his identity blurring. He knew he couldn't have done this. This has to be another elaborate cover up. Bryan realized he was going to be used as a way to explain the rise in recent attacks.

The detectives left Bryan alone with his thoughts, their grim expressions etched in his mind. Bryan sat in the chilling silence, the weight of the accusations pressing down on him. He began to question his own sanity, his own reality.

Could he have been so consumed by his obsession with the creatures of Whispering Pines that he had turned into the very monster he wanted to expose? The question echoed in his mind, a haunting reminder of the fine line between obsession and madness.

As the cell door closed behind him, Bryan was left with his thoughts and the damning evidence against him. Has Bryan become the very monster he was hunting, or is this just another cover up? The truth remained elusive, the answers he sought buried in the depths of the unknown.

And so, the tale of Bryan and the town of Cedarville issued its cautionary message to all who would listen. It served as a haunting reminder that sometimes the pursuit of truth comes at a great cost, leaving one trapped in a web of uncertainty. Bryan's story stood as a warning to those who dared to seek the truth, urging them to consider the consequences of their actions, for in the darkness, the price of knowledge may be higher than anyone could ever imagine.

And in that moment, the legacy of Cedarville and its enigmatic Whispering Pines State Park lived on, etching their names in the annals of mystery, forever reminding the world of the dangers that lie in the pursuit of truth.

Milton Keynes UK
Ingram Content Group UK Ltd.
UKHW020732161023
430697UK00016B/761